KORIN'S CHRONICLES
DEFEATING IDOLIZED, ADULTEROUS LOVE

WALTER LEE

WESTBOW
PRESS®
A DIVISION OF THOMAS NELSON

WestBow Press books may be ordered through booksellers or by contacting:

WestBow Press
A Division of Thomas Nelson & Zondervan
1663 Liberty Drive
Bloomington, IN 47403
www.westbowpress.com
1 (866) 928-1240

ISBN: 978-1-5127-8794-8 (sc)
ISBN: 978-1-5127-8793-1 (hc)
ISBN: 978-1-5127-8795-5 (e)

Library of Congress Control Number: 2017907874

Print information available on the last page.

WestBow Press rev. date: 08/24/2017

INTRODUCTION

My story is not theology or a source of exegetical studies. I pray that you would enjoy this story for what it is: a fictional story that has some Christian theology.

LOTA stands for Love of the Ages, while the subtitle *Defeating Idolatrous, Adulterous Love* can form the acronym DIAL. I did not intend to make the latter acronym, and this book is not a guidebook to killing idolatry. Better books for that are the Bible and *Overcoming Sin and Temptation*, a collection of three of John Owen's helpful works. Lastly, the first letters of the chapter titles including the "E" in "Epilogue" were intentionally made to spell, "Rejoice." This is so that I may remind myself to always rejoice in the self-sufficient Lord.

I finished my first draft as catharsis for getting over a love interest during my junior year of high school, but much later I decided to have fun with my story and revise it. Nonetheless, many parts of my original (but not first because I cannot remember how many times I changed things) draft remain. As a result, *Korin's Chronicles* is a story I cannot write today, for the person I am while writing this introduction is different from the person I was while writing the previous drafts. The latter is immature, so Korin, who is based on my past self, starts out immature in some ways, but please be patient with him as he matures over the course of this book.

I thank the Christian triune God for the grace He has given me.

It is because of Christ redeeming me first that I can seek God in a personal relationship and rejoice in all circumstances. In Christ alone, I enjoy creation and creating and so glorify God.

I thank my parents who have suffered much for and loved over a brat like me, my older sister, my family, my pastor, my spiritual mentor, friends, church, and, as my sixth grade teacher said, all the little people along my path.

I now offer my imperfect book to the one perfect, omnipresent God, trusting that He will use my inferior words for His superior plan. I now give to you, dear reader, my thanks for your time. May you enjoy, and may grace be with you!

Dedicated to God

Reality

Unsatisfied with his test against Job, Satan said to God, "Man alone cannot come close to Christ's perfection, but suppose a Man had help from a Spirit, and you, O God, blessed the Man. The Man would form a new Trinity: a human, a Spirit, and a blessing of God. How would that turn out? Would he not turn against you? I would like to test this on Korin Hugo, the Observer."

God consented but forbid Satan from killing His child unless the child kills himself, and so the beginning and end ensue.

Korin contemplated suicide at the age of four because he believed that he was worthless. People bullied him, saying that he is a waste of breath and the reason why dogs died, why his family is poor, and why others are unhappy. He started criticizing himself to sleep every night, telling himself that someone even a little more important than him deserved to breathe the air he breathed. He waited every night for his parents and older sister to fall asleep so that he could stab his heart with the kitchen knife, but he was afraid of feeling pain. He criticized his fear as cowardly, saying that his feelings and opinions did not matter.

Each night, however, he fell asleep before his parents did. One night, he grew so tired of living that he did not lie down until his parents fell asleep. In spite of his fear, he decided that it was time to die. He thought, however, that if he was going to end it all, one more day would not be any harm. He wondered if anybody except for his family would go to his funeral. He wondered why he had no friends. He told himself that the answer was because he was worthless. He reflected on how he kept making mistakes, not realizing that everyone makes mistakes. If something went wrong, he told himself that it was because he failed to do something or did something bad. Then he remembered his parents. His mother, Hanul Hugo, had said she loves him very much and that he should become a man who takes care of her. His father, Wright Hugo, had said that he wishes he could stay with him forever. Korin knew by their actions and words that they were telling the truth. While he secretly told himself that he was worthless, his parents said that he was precious. He started to cry, but when he imagined his parents crying over his dead body, he grieved. He told himself that he was selfish for wanting to live, but he decided to live for his parents without realizing that this was unselfish.

He then wondered what the purpose of his life was. He loved his parents, but he wondered if there was something more. He wondered what would happen if he and his parents and older sister, Lun Hugo, were all sick. He realized that nobody would take care of them, but he looked out his room window and saw the trees. He wondered how nature and everything came to be, and he marveled at how everything seemed to be part of Someone's plan. He did not yet know God, but he asked towards the ceiling if Someone would make itself known to him. He felt comforted as though Someone was listening, but he was confused by the silence.

A few days later, Lun's friend invited his family to church, where he heard about the Son of God, Jesus. Someone had a name: Jesus Christ. He rejoiced! He was glad that Jesus cares for his family, but he thought that nobody would die for him. Each night, however, he prayed to God, and he felt the Holy Spirit inaudibly assure him, 'I love you.' He felt love and peace, but he was afraid that his mind was trying to make himself feel better. He knows now, however, that he could not have made himself feel better because up to that point he had only brought himself further to believe that he was worthless and closer to suicide. He knows that the triune God saved him.

Though he does not remember much else from his first six years, he remembers his conversion. The pain of unwanted loneliness was too agonizing to forget, and it would only be saved by the good news that Jesus died an even more excruciating death to provide the special grace of forgiving all the sins of those who repent and believe by faith that he is the resurrected Son of God who will return a second time.

Junior, that is, a boy in his junior year of high school, sits in Drama class, observing posters of movies and encouraging quotes tacked on the dead walls while people chatter around him. He wishes to look up at the clouds, but the ceiling blocks them out.

He looks around at his classmates, self-righteously judging them in his immaturity and despondency, yet he notices what few others do, particularly one girl whose cuts still show on her wrists. The Observer sees people, whose bodies are like stringed victims of the needle of loneliness. The needle pricks emotions, stitches forced smiles, and causes some to cut their own skin and sew elaborate adornments to cover their marks. It allows the stringed victims to strengthen with hope during the day, only to cruelly poke their sparkling eyes dry of tears by night. The lonely strings endure this cycle in and out of life's fabric until their strings are cut and corpses fall. The Observer empathizes with them, senses their pains, and suffers alongside them in their secrets, but none empathize with him.

The Observer shrugs and takes out a script in the final minutes before lunch. He covers his ears for silence and reads the packet he had typed up last night. On the top right corner are the words: Korin Hugo. In the script, a captain calms down a guest and asks him to recall a sound. Korin puts down the script and pretends to be the guest with his own answers. He closes his eyes and listens to a laughter full of hearts. The Captain asks to recall a word. Away. Korin opens his eyes brimming with tears, but everyone is too self-absorbed to notice him. Love is eternal, yet her love, if love is mortal, had faded.

As he exits the building, he passes a stone table and anticipates the sound.

"Hola, Korin!" she jokingly calls.

He looks at his friend, Marsha Ruth, a tan girl, and smiles. He had to put away his books, but the main reason why he went this way rather than a second path away from the table, is to hear Marsha greet him. He prays that the triune God would save her from her atheistic beliefs and appreciates her for who she is: a kind friend.

"H-Hello," Korin stutters in a playful accent.

They exchange witty remarks and laugh. Silence. Her friends are talking amongst themselves, but Korin stands, uncertain of what to say, so they exchange a tacit smile as he walks away. He does not like saying farewell.

"Wait," she says as Korin's heart jumps. "You still need to tell me about *HER*."

Korin shivers and says, "Yes, master."

"Stop calling me master."

"Yes, empress," he says. He calls her that because he had read the ESV Bible verses, 1 Peter 2:16-17: "Live as people who are free, not using your freedom as a cover-up for evil, but living as servants of God. Honor everyone. Love the brotherhood. Fear God. Honor the emperor." He understands that it is about honoring everyone as if each person is an emperor. He interprets the verse literally and references it in order to elicit laughter in others whenever someone tells him to do something, but also to help people realize how unintentionally demanding their words sound. He smiles at Marsha and walks away, but now his mind is on *HER*. She had suddenly left him without explanation. It had been a year and six months since they had first fallen in love at first sight, but he cannot recover from the loss of his first love. He had asked Marsha to help him get over *HER*, but Marsha had no advice.

He returns to the library and reads. Reading is second nature to him.

He walks to his next class in which he usually enjoys learning, but his mind is not in the mood. He swirls the water in his bottle, watching a whirlpool form until he stops and lets the water return to normal, but not without bubbles that slowly pop to nothing. He looks at his English teacher. Three weeks ago, Korin learned about existentialism. Now his teacher was describing the complexities of African culture to prove that Africans are not the simple savages described in Conrad's *Heart of Darkness*.

The bell rings, and Korin exits the class in Building C. He sees Marsha across the hall, but he quickly walks away, leaving his heart in the hall. He turns to a second exit and avoids looking back, but each step away is a fading heartbeat until he stops and turns around. The soft pulse grows stronger as he takes a step towards the bench she always stops by. A crowd of people makes it difficult to see her as he takes another step forward. His heart feels warmer with his third step despite the winter air. He smiles as he sees her through the crowd, but she is looking up at a boy. Her eyes closed, her arms enamored around the boy's neck, her lips reaching for his. Korin observes her happiness in the cold. He feels hollow, hearing the absence of his heart, which lies on the hallway floor, where no one is walking.

Korin walks to his next class, cursing himself for liking someone who already had a boyfriend. He did not know that she had a relationship when his interest in her sparked. She told him too late, and by then the love had already flamed. He tries to work in the last class of the day, but his mind is lost. He hoped to start anew with Marsha and forget *HER*.

He remembers how he intended to walk around the cities to look for *HER* but had chosen not to due to schoolwork. He cannot wait any longer. His impulse is to indulge in his pain by walking as far away from anything even remotely familiar. He knows his pain is stupid. There are darker pains in the world, horrors he cannot imagine in sanity, yet here he is, mourning a single heartbreak. One year and six months of heartbreak over *HER*, and suddenly he cannot handle another one over Marsha. He growls inside, thinking how pathetic he is. He must go into the night, far away from comfort, and deeper within his hollow chest. He must amplify his pain to quench his psychological suffering of being constrained in society. He must suffer more of anything but self-harm to forget his current sorrow and discover the core pain inside of him, but society restrains his ability to explore. Freedom. He needs freedom from the world. Here in the classroom, he sits to avoid trouble, but he must find true freedom for several days and delve in his sorrow before he can return for his heart in the hallway. The bell rings for the last time before winter break, and Korin leaves last.

Korin's mother drives to a halt half an hour past promptness despite her lack of profession. He growls and leans back on the front seat as they exit the parking lot. Korin glares at the rushing road ahead and observes a pedestrian to his right. His mother scolds him for his attitude, but he covers his left ear. She yells with more ferocity, but Korin is thinking about the pedestrian. School is Korin's only goal so far because it is required of him by law; it limits him from the life of a pedestrian.

His mother parks, and Korin walks to the second story of his apartment where he contemplates on his bed, while his mother is still reaching the outdoor stairs. He does not know where he would walk to, but he knows he must go. He wants to leave his annoying mother, but he still loves the old woman.

Korin reads a book about the psychology of habits, but his mother barges in and yells at him to study. She has nagged him for three months about retaking a college exam he had passed, for she wanted him to get a better score. She forbid him from other activities and woke him up when he slept before midnight, complaining that he will never become anything by being a top ten student instead of the valedictorian. Korin reads, while she tires herself out and leaves. Korin pushes her insults out of his mind and sleeps.

Korin walks to a familiar door and opens it to a small, dark room. It is the room where he used to rendezvous with *HER* every week. He drops to his knees, mouth agape in shock. Goose bumps tingle throughout his body as he looks at *HER* walk towards him. He is crying silently.

"You're going to be all right," she says, patting his head. She returns to the dark to sleep.

Korin awakens in his room and touches his tearless face. The time is 2:24 AM. Depression overflows. Treasured memories, particularly the memory of his first encounter with *HER*, compress his mind in recollection.

"Chase me," she says.

"What?"

"Chase me."

"Uhmm...okay."

She runs slowly and looks back to reassure herself that she has not been abandoned. Her eyes sparkle with delight when she sees him walking toward her, and she runs faster as the walls echo her gorgeous laughter. In two minutes, she stops across the church cross with her hand held up to silently ask for a break. She is panting heavily, her shoulders drooping in exhaustion, but her eyes shine with content. She sets up two folding chairs side by side, sits, and timidly pats the other chair as if afraid that he would leave. Korin sits to fulfill her wish.

They talk until she catches her breath and runs around the room again. They would meet every week, looking for each other until the day she would stop acknowledging his presence.

Junior, who had been smiling fondly, loses his grin amongst the leaks from his eyes as his mind returns to the grim present. Korin observes the dark, oppressive ceiling that blocks the sky.

Korin stands as he hears a ringing. He reaches over to a device he did not know he had and watches a little girl in a live video, staring at him through a tablet. She smiles and holds up a white board that reads "Jujube." She mouths the word but makes no sound, smiling earnestly and then drawing an image of a bearded Jesus. The video tilts. The girl is shrouded by men in black clothes, but she still smiles at him until the screen dies. Korin cries as he realizes he knows her somehow. He reaches for a phone but awakens in his room alone. A dream. Korin relaxes as he reflects. He does not own an electronic tablet, yet in his mind the dream was so real that he believed he had one. He persuades himself that the dream has no significance of real events, but he assumes that the girl is a victim of sex trafficking who had given her last message to him. Korin remains puzzled over why the girl had contacted him of all people and what she means by "Jujube," but his eyelids grow heavy.

He walks down the stairs to the living room where some neighbors are conversing until a young girl runs through the door and speaks to a male pastor. Korin is unacquainted with many of his neighbors, but he knows that the pastor has a cousin who traveled out to evangelize. The pastor's cousin is a kind girl who Korin enjoys talking to. She gave him a cake once, saying he should eat it and many other goods to get fatter. She smiled at him, and Korin, who usually denies sweets, accepted her heartfelt gift and ate the cake. Korin's heart sinks, sensing news before he hears it. The pastor stands, swaying slightly as the room grows silent.

"My cousin is dead."

The pastor's wife buries her face in her hands, and Korin awakens again. He rushes out of bed and realizes he is in his own room. The time is too early for even the pastor downstairs to awaken for his early morning devotions. Korin drowsily returns to his room and collapses. *A missionary works for God and dies for God*, he thinks. *Thank goodness I'm not God. How does He choose? Does He choose to save his faithful servant, or does He sacrifice the servant as a scapegoat in order to save the strangers and show them true love? Well, there is Christ, so I might know God's answer. What would I have chosen? I do not know. I want the cousin to come back; she is a sweet girl who should not have to die, but if it means saving several people.... I do not know, but God, if you are listening, I want her to come back alive, please. I want her to live. I do not know about the others, but I want her to live.*

Korin shivers and covers himself with blankets. *Everything is dark and heartless.* He moves in his bed, reluctant to have more dreams in which he is helpless to help people. He does not understand these dreams, but he does not ask God due to his fear of what he may learn, so he disregards the visions as mysterious memories his tired mind unconsciously mashed together with no importance. He persuades himself, albeit partially, that he simply misses the pastor's cousin, but the thought comforts him to sleep.

Korin dreams once more, this time of a tranquil island that seems both familiar and novel, filled with a sense of romantic possibility in an unknown land. There is a pyramid and an open quad formed by brown bricks. Shrubs are growing between the cracks, gasping for life amidst a forest of bulky, green trees and an expanse of mountains looming over desolated ruins. He walks past the arched stone entrance, which suddenly shakes. Straight ahead, Korin sees a volcano erupt; the bricks crack, and lava oozes down the mountains, smothering the pyramid in its fiery spit. Korin suddenly notices three people who seem to accompany him, and they grab ancient, golden shields lying beside them. One of them hands Korin a shield, and they use the shields as sleds down a group of stairs to the ocean shores. Korin cannot float in water or swim far distances because he swallows water whenever he turns his head up for air, so he is grateful for their support. They approach a gap of thirty-five meters with a calm ocean between two smooth boulders the size of three stories. The countless waves molded the boulders and formed one hole the size of two stories in each boulder. Two companions are almost at the other side, while the third companion is behind Korin. Korin enters the water without fear, considering how his two companions had waded through with little difficulty, but his third step finds no foundation as he plummets into the ocean, light blue and hazy. He sees a figure with glowing eyes approximately sixty meters away from shore. Korin perceives the shape to be that of a giant turtle or tortoise, which watches him silently as Korin slams his hands and kicks the space beneath his feet to cross the short distance to the opposite rock. Korin gasps for air and sits on the hole of the boulder while his third companion wades halfway through the gap with ease. Suddenly, the shape of the giant creature is at the shore, but the third companion has crossed in time to join Korin at the boulder and escape with the other two people.

Korin looks once more at the ceiling. His drowsy eyes see the clock read 5 AM. Korin reflects in astonishment at the size of the tortoise and its glowing eyes that made it seem like an entity in his dream. Korin walks to his apartment door and decides to walk about his neighborhood. He hopes to see the sunrise as he contemplates upon his dreams. He puts on a chrome jacket and exits the apartment.

He is a knight guarding his secret visions while searching for more secrets, unknown Holy Grails to behold.

Later that Saturday afternoon, Korin walks several miles to attend a crafts service for the elderly in a retirement home and avoid a car ride with his mother.

At the service, he tries to talk to an elderly woman, but she just glares at the table.

"She can't speak English because she knows only French."

Korin looks at a different old woman who smiles widely at him. "What's your name?

"Korin Hugo."

"Corn?"

"Korin."

"Oh, that's an interesting name. What does it mean?"

"I am not quite sure why my parents named me that, but they must have liked the phonetics. I looked at the dictionary and discovered that Korin means 'the best thing to ever happen to me.' My last name means 'bright in mind and spirit' and 'intelligence.' There have been foundations set before my existence, but perhaps now I will walk on these foundations, such as the ones Christ set for me with his sacrifice so that I may reach out to people, and walk on my own curious road ahead."

"That's good. I remember my own road. When I was in Germany, I spoke German, but now everyone seems to speak English instead. Anyways, I was once like her" she says as she gestures towards the gloomy woman. "I couldn't speak English, but during World War II, I met an American soldier. My mom didn't want me to be with him, but I was happy, so she decided to let me keep the relationship. The war ended, and I married the man and had a kid, and by then my mother had migrated to America because she had wanted to stay as far away as possible from the battle. I stayed because Germany was my home, and my husband was still stationed there at the time. Then, my mother said she could get me a green card to come over, and I said, 'Well, wait mom. I need to talk with my husband,' so I told him and we agreed to go. My son—he was about six years old at the time—was ecstatic," she says with a chuckle. "He kept telling me that he couldn't believe they were going to America, and once we had reached my mother's home, my son kept searching for houses for lease so that we could move out to our own home. He found one at the end of the same street my mother lived in, and my family moved out, but he found another house in the middle of that street, so we moved again."

"How is your family now?"

"My husband passed away four years ago." She nods at Korin's empathetic eyes and says, "Yes, I know. My son is a leader in charge of the city's Board of Education."

"Really?" Korin says, impressed.

"Yes, but right now he and his wife are probably on a trip somewhere. They visit me sometimes. You should come back the next time we have these crafts events."

"I'll try to come back."

"You are very handsome. What was your name again?"

"Korin."

"Ah, yes, that's right. Well, what shall we make today?"

Korin punctures the top of a Styrofoam cup so that a string fits through with tiny bells that would ring when hung on a door that is then opened. He looks at his interlocutress and hesitates to ask for her age in fear of disrespecting her. Her veins form a maze beneath her wrinkled skin on her arms.

"Oh, that's beautiful," she says. "Thank you for making this for me. I'll write my name here."

As she writes on the cup, Korin inquires, "Is this your favorite place?"

"Oh, yes. The people here are nice; they feed me. We watch movies; we play Bingo on Fridays. Bingo is such a nice game. I've won many times."

"You don't miss Germany?"

"No, I like it here. Germany is nice, but this is where my family is now, so I stay here in America."

She hums a tune and twirls the Styrofoam Cup hanging by a string. The soft rendition is barely audible but full of hearts flowing in his ears. "I know that song."

"You do? It's a nice song, isn't it?"

"Moon River."

"Yes," she affirms with an appreciative smile, one that breeds from familiarity.

She begins to hum a little louder now that at least one person accepts her voice. She sings some of the lyrics in a lovely voice, nicely paired with her nostalgic gaze that looks back upon the many years of her life until then.

Korin smiles and asks, "Do you know who Audrey Hepburn is?"

"Why, yes! She was a lovely woman."

"What movies have you seen her in?"

"I saw her in *Breakfast at Tiffany's*. I like that one. I don't think I've seen her in anything else."

"Have you seen *Roman Holiday*?"

"No, but I think I've heard of it. I'm not sure. Who is in it?

"Gregory Peck."

"Ah, well I'm not sure I saw that. I have been to Italy, though. I was lost there. I met Ernest Hemingway. He's a good author."

"You did?" he responds, alarmed.

"Yes. He was walking around in Italy, and I asked him if he could help me find directions, but we ended up sitting on a bench on the intersection where we talked for hours. He said he was on one of his ordinary walks, and I was surprised when he told me his name.

I knew he was an author, but I didn't know him too well. He was a nice man to talk to."

"Do you know F. Scott Fitzgerald?"

"No, I don't think so."

By then, other volunteers had left, having fulfilled their hours. They left immediately, leaving Korin with Sophia.

"You're an interesting boy. How old are you now?"

"Sixteen."

"You are so young and tall. It's very nice that you have interests. It makes you interesting. Do you know what you want to do?"

"I want to become an author."

"Oh, as in books. How exciting. You should have a scenario that no one expects so that they get interested. Are you working on one now?"

"Not quite."

"Well, it will be hard to live that life. It won't be easy to get food through that job."

"Yes."

"But don't let that get you down. I'm sure you'll work something out."

Korin looks at the clock; he had stayed twenty-three minutes past the end time of the volunteer event and feels uncertain about when he should go back to his apartment, but he feels at home with Sophia.

"You've been a nice person to listen to me. I hope things go well for you, Korin. You should come join me; it's lunch time."

"I think I should be getting back to my apartment. My mom might be worried if I don't."

"Oh, okay. You'll come back next time?"

"Yes."

"Here, I have plenty of crafts in my room; I want you to have this. You made it after all."

"I'm not so sure if I should take it. I made it for you."

"This is my gift to you then. Thank you for coming."

Korin accepts the Styrofoam doorbell, smiles, and waves farewell. He walks back to his apartment.

Encounter

Korin's mother slams the apartment door open. He explains that he made a wind chime out of a cup, strings, and bells for an elder who gave it to him during community service. His mother degrades him as a failure who will never marry. He remembers *HER* and walks to his room with his mother tailing him. He warns her to leave, but she bursts out insults. Korin pushes her out of his room and into the living room against a mirror. He steps back in shock at his cruel expression, but he turns away. Korin's mother looks at him with shock and runs after him, but he shuts his door and pushes against it, against his mother's will as she pounds the door. She screams in misery and calls her husband. She knocks on the door and says he wants to talk to Korin. Korin opens the door and listens to threats against his life if Korin stays in the apartment. His father hangs up.

Korin looks across his small room at a backpack he had filled with provisions if he ever had to leave in an emergency.

It is six in the evening, two hours before his father returns from work, so Korin quickly packs more clothes in his luggage. His mother had left to buy groceries and calm down. He feels sick, but he quickly overcomes the emotion with a sense of liberty. He had intended to leave his apartment before, but he finally determines that today is when the tension of his societal bonds snaps. His mind knows not where to go, but he is certain he must move towards somewhere new.

His church is in the right direction, but he wants to avoid potential recognition, so he moves in the direction he knows best: to the left towards school, where no one would care about his presence. He leaves his phone at the apartment so that he is completely free of communication; he needs to live, to walk, to breathe, to feel. Drivers look at him curiously as if he is some anomaly. Korin's back begins to ache while his legs weaken due to his previous walks, but he presses on, mind feeling fresh and fearless of other pedestrians in the dark or any form of legality stopping his walk. He had walked this path before by choice, but the sense of liberty was degraded by the assurance that he had a shelter to return to. Now, he indulges in his freedom so much that he decides to find an alternate path to take as he turns to a pitch black, desolate park on a road not taken. He remembers how he had avoided the dreaded look of the path, and even now his heart beats quicker, yet his feet move forward; they must keep going.

A man stands by the only lamp near the park with his dog, and both peer at Korin, the pedestrian. They anticipate danger until Korin simply walks into the spotlight to prove his innocence. The man says, "Good evening," demanding Korin to speak and assure him that Korin is friendly, so Korin gently responds the like. Once Korin passes them, the master and dog continue to play, but as Korin enters a neighborhood street, he looks back with silent panic. The man is walking in his direction with the dog by his side. Korin turns right and runs as quietly and quickly as possible, frightened that the dog might catch his scent. His legs are burning, so he rests at the end of the street while the luggage on his back pulls him towards earth.

He trudges on and focuses on his surroundings, on the houses he had not seen before as he feels like a foreigner in another world within his world. He sees through the windows shadows flying like the

Reaper himself. Bright, open garages reveal lives he knows nothing about, but are as real as his own. Korin marvels as each glance gives him some information about the character of each homeowner. He wants to see if anyone would shelter him, but he doubts anyone will, judging by the looks people give him from their garages as he walks by. They see him as some potential criminal and look away only when Korin is seven houses away. Korin does not care. He simply wants to live, but he wants life to last. He wonders whether he should just go to the beach and enjoy the scenery until he starves to death. It is much better to live than to exist, to enjoy rather than to survive. He reasons that he would truly live once death is imminent. Then, Korin realizes he can die at any moment by some unfortunate occurrence. He wonders if that means life is better experienced by enjoying every second. His mind continues to ponder while his feet return to the main street, where mechanical beasts rush by.

A new wave of cars zooms by, and fear strikes Korin. He worries about where to sleep, what to eat, how to get a job, and anything that requires his identification or parental approval; he realizes that he is still trapped. His walk is just a taste of desired freedom, an illusory sample of the greater truth of complete solitude. Korin crosses the street and wonders about his parents but quickly retaliates in repulsion. Little does Korin know that his imperfect parents love him, and that his mother would cry to see that her only son is gone with no way for her to contact him.

A book drops. Korin stops and sets down his bag, open from the weight of his possessions pulling down the zipper. He takes out several books from his bag, now significantly lighter at the price of his hands' freedom as he holds his books.

BEEP! A middle-aged kid hoots while sticking his head out a car window, startling Korin to irritation. At the next intersection, drivers coldly stare at him and his two bags, but Korin presses on. He reflects that some people are ignorant, rather than cruel. He calms down from his anger, telling himself that there is usually a reason to sympathize with a person or action, often something beyond a thing in itself, and that he has been forgiven much by God and so ought to forgive others.

He then reaches the street his parents had always entered to reach their old neighborhood. It is the only home he recalls, for he did not remember moving from Korea to California as an infant, but he sees no reason to go to his old home. Korin presses on towards his school. He pauses. He has no reason to go anywhere, so there would be no harm done if he spent time reminiscing the past. It has only been forty minutes since he had left, too soon for his parents to notice his absence and look for him, so he turns into the neighborhood. There is no sound but his tired steps and steady breathing. The mechanical beasts are away in the main street, and the ones in the neighborhood are asleep; peace arises. As Korin passes by a lamp, it flashes then darkens. Korin wonders if that is a sign of God, that he should turn back before he crosses the Rubicon, or that he is going the right way to peace away from manmade light, towards the natural world. He would finally achieve solitude, he decides, and the death of the lamp, a part of society, means that he is closer to new life true to his inherent nature of freely roaming the world.

Korin stops in front of the house, outcast from the sanctuary of his childhood. It had been repainted over in dark brown since he last saw it. He sits in front of the old garden. It is hollower than he had remembered, even though the new owners had planted grass. It is all familiar novelty. With his bags on the floor, Korin stretches his arms and looks up to the sky. A ceiling of pollution blocks the stars. Nonetheless, the sky is limitless. He waits for God. He has no purpose, yet his stomach growls for sustenance, always wanting more for the flesh. The day before, Korin did not finish his lunch, so he packed his apple slices that afternoon as a final feast, the last before he would eat his canned goods over time. He treasures this temporary meal and wonders about going back the way he came towards church where he could get more food and possibly live there in secret, but the risks of being seen by acquaintances is too high for him. Korin bites the tip of one skinny slice, the bursts of flavor packing his taste buds. Korin finishes the slice and packs his food away, deciding he can eat slightly rotten apples over the next few days while the cans and his monetary savings can last him about two months with his frugal choices. He is ready to live and die.

Korin moves away from the house and walks to a park at the edge of the street where he rests on a bench. Darkness. He recalls how his sister had begged him to walk back to back with her, their arms interlaced, whenever she entered their parents' dark room in their previous home. Once she turned on the lights, she would tell him to leave. She would close the bathroom door before he could return to the bright hallway. He slowly became accustomed to the dark, shut out from light, but now he is outdoors, unable to return to a warm, lit hallway.

He looks up at the starless skies as he lies down on the stone bench. He stares at his childhood jungle gym with fondness. He had climbed it the few times he visited, reaching the top and seeing the world below. Conversely, life had grown bigger in difficulty, and the jungle gym now seemed small. "I can think about tomorrow later and sleep today. Today's worries are enough for their day."

These words are ripples distorting the body of calm water in time. They thin out over time until forgotten by the mortal mind, but Korin is a mortal Observer who remembers. This Observer senses the dying ripples before the pure reflection of the water, of time, is restored to the way it was before the interruption, though with some new effects from the ripples. The Observer, having felt the interruption, further appreciates the calm waters. The interruption. A ripple—an age—of five days in one night.

Korin is sinking in darkness. He feels calm as a cold, transparent substance shrouds him, blanketing him in a curious sense of warmth and remembrance within his mind. He is breathing somehow in the liquid-like substance. Korin looks up at a sliver of light and senses he is not alone. He looks below at fishes and creatures swimming in separate communities, oblivious of life elsewhere. Korin notices that he can see better, looks up, and barely sees two sources of light arriving together before he raises his hand to cover his eyes. He turns around towards the creatures that seem to continue with their existences, but Korin realizes that they are still.

"Excuse me."

Korin slowly opens his eyes and flinches when he sees a moving figure, whose face is shadowed beneath a street light, which he assumes had turned on during his sleep. He sits up, head aching as he blinks rapidly away from the light before observing the details of the stranger's countenance. His heart leaps several beats; shivers rain down his back as he gazes aghast. A young woman curiously watches him with kind, brown eyes. He knows her name.

"Hello," she elegantly says without effort but with concern, "are you all right?

Korin reaches for his bags, while his eyes trace her presence in case she disappears, but he feels cold wood instead. He continues to lie back down to avoid appearing lost for reaching towards nothing, though he sees in her kind eyes how silly his fear is. Korin feels his cheek touch the bench, which fully awakens him to notice it is not the same stone bench he slept on. He realizes his gaping mouth is awestruck and consciously forces it shut.

"Fine, yes. Fine I am. I-I am fine."

"May I know why you are here so late in the evening?"

"Late," he mutters. "Well...walking, and then sat...my legs...I slept."

"Would you like me to call a taxi for you?" she asks politely.

"That's quite all right," Korin says. "My...walking. Feet." Korin stares down, moving his legs to prove his ability to walk, but his vision blurs even with his spectacles, and he loses consciousness from a headache. The woman reaches out with her right hand, stopping Korin's head from falling. He quickly regains focus from the smoothness of her warm hand on his cheek. He sits back up in nervous delight and shakes his head awake. He looks at her eyes, which gaze at him in astonishment.

"If you give me a moment, I can look for someone to take you home."

"No, please. I truly am fine." Korin says urgently. He pauses, recollecting his calm manner as he slowly asks, "May I know why you are here so late in the evening?"

"I was enjoying a walk through the garden. It's rather pleasant to visit nature in its purity yet still be near a comfortable home. Do you think that makes sense?

"Absolutely, but this isn't a garden. It's my childhood park. Do you always help people sleeping on benches?"

She laughs and replies, "No, you're an exception. I don't recall seeing a young man sleeping this late at night on a bench, but I suppose one can marvel at a place like this and peacefully fall asleep amidst such wonders."

Korin smiles at her and realizes there is something peculiar about the lamp, which was off when he fell asleep. He does not recall how the lamp looked, but he is almost certain that it did not have a case around it. He sees more trees than usual, and there is no playground where he had occasionally played during his childhood. The street where his old home was is gone. His eyes wander as his interlocutress steps forward.

"Are you sure you are all right?"

"Not quite anymore. Where am I?"

"Why, you're in Rome!"

Korin stands up and wavers in his stance. He is taller than the woman, who tilts her head at him in confusion. He believes he is dreaming and decides to enjoy his time while he can by talking with the interlocutress.

"My apologies. My head is aching for some reason, but I assure you it has nothing to do with carousing; I am not that depressed, and I will never be a drunk. I am just so utterly exhausted, but your kindness refreshes me. How is it that you are so kind?"

"You talk funny. You mistake me, however, for being kind; I just wanted to make sure you were fine when I saw you sleeping in the dark. You do not appear to be homeless or dangerous, so I awoke you. I am sure there are kinder people who would do the same."

"Suppose I was dangerous, you being a young woman and me a crazy man, which I am not, but suppose that is the case. Should you not walk on for your safety and leave me, a potential threat, to sleep and potentially get ill from the cold?"

"I am not sure how to explain why, but somehow I thought you weren't dangerous, and that I should help you even if I was scared because you seemed to be in a worse situation. I was scared, though, but I reasoned I could use pepper spray or something."

"Yes, but you want to be careful when you're alone."

"Should I have left you alone?"

"Yes."

"Then we wouldn't be having this conversation."

"Yes, but if I was a monster.... I couldn't stand such a horror."

She smiles and says, "Well, thank goodness that is not the case. My name is—"

Korin responds, "You don't have to tell me your name."

"Oh," she says, taken aback.

"I already know your name, figuratively."

"How do you mean?"

"Well, I don't usually do this. Let's just say you are your own self, and no name should have to define that about you. There are many people who share the same name, but not a single one of them are identical with another, which by all means makes the world more intriguing. Korin stands up and wavers in his stance with a slight headache that disappears as suddenly as it had appeared. He is taller than the woman, who tilts her head at him in confusion. He believes he is dreaming and decides to enjoy his time while he can by talking with her. They greet each other and tell each other their names.

She smiles. "Korin. What an interesting name. What does it mean?"

He explains the meaning but adds, "Then again, that's up to you. What do you think of when you hear my name?"

"Korin, to me your name means a kind, strange, and interesting person to meet in nature."

"In nature?"

"In life."

"Is there a difference?"

"All the difference. In nature you have the world; in life you have many worlds."

"How insightful of you. How does my name mean anything to many worlds?"

"That's up to you," she teases. "By the way, are you new here?"

"To Rome at this time? Yes," he laughs. "Did you ask because I'm Asian?"

"No," she says with a pause, "I've met a few Asians here. You speak differently, but not because of your ethnicity or an accent. I'm not sure how to explain it, but I guess I can say that your voice is unusually delicate, like a melancholic melody."

"And if I am not from here, where do my people come from, these people who speak delicately?" Korin jokes. "I think your voice is very nice, like that of a peaceful lullaby."

"Perhaps we're all scattered about the world from all sorts of people."

"Scattered about many worlds."

"Yes, in life."

"And in nature?"

"We are just a small part in nature, the big scope of the universe."

"Ah, you mean the galaxy?"

"Yes, I look up at the skies and wonder about the stars."

Korin looks up with her, admiring the worlds above. He looks at the woman's sparkling eyes reflecting an awe of the heavens and lives unknown. She turns to smile at him, showing him an equal if not absolute awe of the lives known. She shivers and says, "If you don't have a place to stay, would you like to visit my apartment? I doubt you mean any harm, and I'm sure you are a caring person."

"What makes you so sure? I mean, I don't want to hurt you, and it's such a pleasure to meet you, but how can you tell if that's true when we just met?"

She smiles and laughs, "It's not hard to tell if someone cares about you." Korin blushes as she adds, "Then again, I suppose it is more difficult to know why someone cares, so why do you care about my safety?"

"Well, I don't want someone to be in danger with a stranger, but I care even more about your safety because you are a kind person. I'm glad that you cared enough to wake me up, check to see if I was okay, and offer me shelter," he says as he regrets pushing his mother. "I don't deserve that kindness, though, so I'll just stay here."

"Well, there you have it. You care about my safety for my benefit, not your own, even if that means you have to stay in the cold, but you see," she says with a smile, "according to you, I'm a kind person, and as a kind person, I don't want you to stay out in the cold."

Korin stares at her kind yet determined eyes and laughs. "Thank you."

Music spreads through the night from down by the water where people party together. Korin smiles at the sounds and dancers, and when the woman sees him, she gently holds his hand and gestures towards the water.

"Oh, no," he says. "I can't dance."

"You don't know for sure unless you try."

"Oh, I know."

"You need to open up more. I'm sure you have it in you somewhere if you just feel the rhythm and dance," she says with a little jump.

Korin refuses but is running with her as he hears the music more, the cool air flying to his face and his right hand warm against her right hand, her sonorous laughter encouraging him to catch up towards the lights shining upon the dark, blue water.

"I thought you were tired."

"So did I!" she says joyously, and they race off while the night is young.

Soon they reach the lively party and pant. A band plays music as people dance, and one male grows interested and asks to dance with the woman. Korin respectfully stands back and watches them dance within the crowd. Korin is content that she is beaming and occasionally looking at him instead of her dance partner. Most of the guys begin to notice her, but she keeps looking at Korin as if he alone is there, always failing to hold back a grin in return. The song ends, and the woman graciously thanks her partner so that the male, understanding her kindness, nods appreciatively and leaves as she runs up to take Korin's right hand, dragging him to the middle of the platform just as the next song commences.

"You're dancing," she exclaims.

"I'm moving my feet."

"You're moving to the rhythm."

"I'm copying that guy behind you."

"Here, may I guide you?"

"Yes."

She moves his left hand with hers and moves his right hand to her back as he involuntarily flinches. She laughs and places her right hand on his left shoulder, guiding his steps until he learns to move on his own with her in a few minutes. Once Korin learns the moves, having danced before in his Spanish class, the woman asks him to take the leader position while she follows in the dance. He knows that she can lead better than he can because she knows the moves better, but she says that she feels more comfortable being the follower in the dance while a man leads her. They work together, however, because the follower is just as important as the leader, for there is no leader without a follower. Despite his awkwardness, she sees him as a loving leader.

"There, it's all simple. We'll try a quick Merengue."

"A what?"

"I'll help you." She lets go of his right hand and rhythmically swirls, gently moving his hand above and around her head, then picks up his right hand to do the same motion but with his opposite hand. She guides him through the moves until he soon gets the motions in his mind, and they dance more smoothly as she laughs each time his eyes light up in recognition of the feelings of each step.

"There, you're getting the hang of it!"

Korin looks around, but she turns his chin to her and says, "They have their own moves. Let's have fun with ours." He smiles and nods, dancing with her until the end of the song but always looking deep into her eyes.

The two sit with their feet hanging above the water, watching the reflection of the moon and laughing. Korin looks at the woman who seems about twenty-three years old. He wonders if she would be frightened by the thought that he is seven years younger than her, let alone that he could be dreaming of the past. He knows it would be best to tell her the truth, at least while the dream lasts.

"I have to tell you something," he says close beside her so that she could hear him over the music.

"Have you found out what it was you thought the moment you first saw me?"

"Not yet."

She looks at his face and says, "What's bothering you?"

"I am seven years younger than you."

"And how old do you think I am?"

He blushes, realizing he did not know for certain her age. "I," he hesitates. "I am not sure."

"Well, if you are sixteen years young, you are correct. You can't be sixteen, though. You look as though you are twenty."

He looks at her silently, his eyes reflecting her red cheeks.

"Oh, but you must be joking." She looks at him, then at the water, then at the stars. "What does it matter?" Her face focuses above as she regains her composure. "We can still be friends, and if what we felt tonight is wrong, then I don't think I can appreciate what is right."

"You are okay with this," he ponders aloud.

"Yes. I haven't enjoyed myself like tonight for some time, and I am sure there are more good moments to come, but it would be a sin to regard this as casual. There are plenty of lovely relationships in which the lovers differ in age, but if their bond is as true as humanly possible, then age should not be a factor."

"I absolutely agree with you. I have read the Bible, and from what I can tell I do not think there is anything against age difference so long as the relationship is kept to glorify God. Still, if I do find something in Scripture that says it is wrong, I may not like the fact, but I will obey it in honor of God. Who am I to say that God is wrong? I need to seek God above everything, for the way to heaven is narrow, and I want to take up my cross and follow God, even if dying to my old self means that I cannot have a relationship with age difference."

"We can be a couple," she says, the water reflecting the red lights on her face. "Does the age difference between us as lovers make us criminals?"

"In your case, I like to say no."

She smiles and slowly looks at him. He notices a sense of fear in her eyes and looks up at the sky. "What if I liked someone much younger than me, or much older than me?" she asks.

"How much?"

"Suppose ten years. Would it be wrong for someone of fifteen years to love a person of five years? Something tells me yes. And what about a boy of ten years in love with a person of twenty years, or our case?"

"I cannot say the same thing about every case, for I do not know the factors involved with each one. I only know about our case," he says as she turns to the moon. "I see what you see—the moon, the stars—but I have my own memories and thoughts associated with these things, and you have yours. Everyone has differing perspectives on the same things. That means not everyone will support love between different ages. All I know is that I'm glad when you're glad, and if you're glad to be away from me, then I'll respect that."

He turns away as she processes the information in her mind, but he shudders when she stands up. His chest feels compressed and hollow, but he sees no expression on his face, billowing in the water below as her reflection ripples away.

Korin looks deep into the water, marveling at how real his dream is while the music continues to liven up the night. He is shocked by how heartlessly calm he appears in the water, while his soul feels torn. He feels as if he had been abandoned by *HER* all over again, and again he is not just alone, but left alone. He wonders if something is wrong with his emotions.

"If you mean what you said, then according to you, you're glad when I'm glad." Korin's skin jumps, and he turns to discover that she had been standing behind him for two minutes but was too far away from the water to be reflected. "According to me, however, I'm glad when I'm with you, but only if you're glad," she says with a grin, "so are you glad?"

Korin smiles back at her. "Yes."

"I want to try," she says.

"You should know one more thing."

"Yes?"

"I think I am dreaming all of this from the future."

"Is that so?" she says.

"I was at a park in America more than sixty years in the future from now, but now I am in Rome."

"I guess that means I love someone about three times my age."

"Yes, I suppose so. My point is, though, that I might not be here for long."

"Will I get to see you again?"

"I hope so."

"Let's go to my apartment before you leave. I would like to get something to eat at home, perhaps some pasta swimming in sauce. I could make you some."

"Yes, please."

The party continues by the water as Korin accompanies the woman to the stairs of her apartment.

"What is the future like?"

"I don't think that would be good of me to tell you."

"Why, if this is a dream, none of it should be real."

"It feels real, though."

"Then perhaps it is. Perhaps you have been dreaming you were from the future and now you've finally waken up to reality."

"No, that can't be."

"Why not?" she ponders. Korin pauses. The woman sees him becoming distressed and exclaims, "Are you serious? You actually...." She shakes the thought out of her mind and checks, "I assure you that we are in the year 1951. I strolled in a garden. We met. Korin, don't worry about this. Dream or no dream, you're here with me now in life, and that's real."

He nods his head, uncertain and relieved, and asks, "Speaking of the future, what do you expect to see in yours?"

"I hope to have a husband," she says, blushing away from Korin, "and I want to give birth to children and raise them in a community where they enjoy their lives. I want to be in their worlds for as long as I can as their loving mother."

Korin pauses. He knows what will happen in her life, and he wants to tell her to avoid a certain man, but he says nothing. He is afraid of unwittingly ruining the lives of others by changing her life and so indirectly changing the lives of others.

"And you, Korin?"

"I want to love my family until my end."

She stares, dazed with her mouth slightly open, as if seeing him in an entirely new light. Korin, amazed by the speechless marvel on her crimson face, smiles. She says, "You make my life interesting."

"I wouldn't go so far as to say your life is a day."

"If today is the happiest day of my life, wouldn't that make today the defining moment of my time here on Earth? In that case, you make my life interesting."

"Surely you have enjoyed your past years as well." Korin regrets saying that, for he remembers reading about her childhood.

"Yes, there have been good moments in my life," she says as she looks down, her focus disappearing into the past, "but none even close to tonight."

"Well, I am honored," he says as she looks up and returns from her thoughts.

"I'll go get the pasta ready now. It won't take long, so please feel free to sit at the couch while you wait."

Korin enters the clean living room and sits on a wooden chair by the table. He feels remarkably comfortable, at peace, and at home.

"Korin, I've been thinking. If I had known of your age the moment I met you, would I have been as affectionate towards you as I am now?"

"You might have taken me to a police station or just taken care of me like a guardian."

"Why shouldn't I be that now, like a guardian instead of a friend?" He looks at her, waiting for her answer. "Well, I don't want to be like a guardian to you," she decides. "That doesn't feel right with me. I'm not taking care of you as though you are my responsibility. I feel like we are companions, people who protect each other, but not in the way that makes us responsible over each other's lives as a good guardian would have to. I don't mean to say that guardians cannot love like friends love, or that a friend's love is greater than that of a guardian. It all depends on the case, but I feel like even the greatest human guardian has an obligation to care for someone. I don't have that obligation, nor would I want to, but I want to oblige you with my friendship."

"If we did know our age gap before all of these events, our relationship would be completely different, wouldn't it?" he responds.

"Yes, I believe so."

"So that means the first encounter is crucial, and that love can happen at first sight."

"Couldn't that mean lust at first sight?"

"Not always. I'm sure skeptics will tell you otherwise, but I'm sure they have the wrong perception of love, too."

"Is it possible that a poor first encounter can be overcome?"

"If you put your heart and complete faith into doing so for God's glory, yes. You can overcome anything with God, and others will eventually see your faith in love and believe in you, too." He sees her smiling in the kitchen as he responds, and they enjoy silence for the next three minutes until she brings out the steaming pasta.

His mouth savors the texture of the sauce smothering the pasta, but still the food disappears all too quickly, as most wonderful things tend to. "Dream or not, this pasta must be on everyone's bucket list of food," he remarks in astonishment. She beams.

Journey

The clock strikes three in the morning as they finish eating. Korin covers his yawn. "Do you have work later today?"

"Yes. I will be tired at six, but I will have the company of kind workers."

They remain in silence for a few seconds as the clock ticks through their unspoken thoughts. She walks to the kitchen sink, occupying herself with the dishes as Korin picks up his plate to wash. "Wait," she blurts out. He recovers from a smile just as she swivels around, flustered. There are no dishes in the sink, but Korin pretends not to notice. "I can take that. Thank you." She looks down away from his eyes and takes the plate with her, while Korin looks around the room. All is desolate in her temporary home, with clean white cupboards under a bright ceiling light, while a separate room to the left of the kitchen holds a washer by a window opened out to the dark world outside. "Does this mean you'll be going, Korin?"

"Huh?" He turns to her as she puts the plate away to avoid eye contact. Korin wonders what to do and cringes. He remembers that he is potentially in a dream, one capable of ending at any moment. His chest echoes a splatter of a drop of pain coursing through his soul in regret. Korin does not know if he will ever dream this again. The dream feels real; Korin feels at peace with life. After a few seconds, the woman unconsciously shifts her feet, so he responds, "I don't have anywhere to go, in this world or my own, but I don't think it would be right for me to sleep here with a single woman, even if we sleep in separate rooms. It would be disrespectful to you if I place myself in a context like this, especially if someone finds out and gossips about this, which reminds me of something. I'm surprised that people didn't recognize you at the dance by the sea."

"Why would they?"

Korin nods and realizes that she is not as famous in 1951 before her film comes out, so he shakes his head. "I mean, who wouldn't want to admire your beauty? Plus, they might have seen some of your past works, so I just thought some fans might have recognized you. Anyways, do you know someplace I could go?"

"How about we just stay up and talk then?"

"I think that's fine if we walk around in a public place. I think it's spiritually dangerous for two people of the opposite gender to stay together in a private space lest love should awaken before its time, that is, before marriage. Aren't you tired, though, especially with work in three hours?"

"That's okay. If you really are dreaming, then I want to enjoy our time together for what it is for however long we have it. Can you wait a few minutes for me to freshen up, though? I might as well get ready for work now."

Korin nods and thanks her. He sits at a comfortable couch and suddenly realizes how tired he is. He wonders about what he would do for work to live if he stays in Rome, or how he would survive in his world. He reflects upon his simple life as an infant cared for by loving parents and wonders about his family. Before he can dwell on his regrets towards his family, he distracts himself. He wonders how the woman can be so kind when her childhood was haunted in Holland during World War II. He had just met the woman, and the year is 1951. She would later suffer an even worse pain, an emotional loss due to two miscarriages. Korin remembers that he had read several biographies about her, how they all speak well of her but call her a biographer's nightmare, for her perpetual kindness made for no scandals to write about. The worst that they could find of the woman was her forgetting to thank her agent during an acceptance speech for an Oscar. In spite of her kindness, she still suffers. Korin wants her to enjoy life, and he remembers that she would finally give birth in 1960. He wants to see her smile at her newborn child, and fatigue shrouds his eyes.

Korin awakens to darkness again, and his heart sinks. *It was all a dream.* He curses himself while his head hurts again, but the pain soon subsides. He knows that common sense says that one cannot suddenly time travel, but he felt each moment—from the touch of her hand to the taste of the pasta—he felt as though, even with common sense, he lived a new reality. He tries to sleep to dream of her again but notices how soft the ground feels. He sits up befuddled and touches a bed instead of the park bench.

He steps on the warm floor and motions through the darkness until he touches a wall and follows it to a door, opening it to see a blurred, gloomy hallway. Korin looks behind him and takes his glasses from a desk, wondering who put them there. He wanders through the quiet corridors, anticipating anything when he is startled by an agonized scream.

Korin looks behind him, wondering if he should leave to the exit sign, but he knows he must see if he can help someone, so he tiptoes down the aisle. Empty space. Each room closed, containing unknown patients. A scream from his right. He reaches the edge of the hall and looks left at more doors. He turns to the right where the hall progressively brightens as he walks barefoot in silence. Fear and sorrow overwhelm him as the screams increase in intensity while he approaches closer to the source. He turns left at the next corner but rushes back behind the wall. A relatively tall man is standing in the middle of the hallway where the screams are coming from. His hands are behind his back, which is facing the corner so that the stranger did not notice Korin. The man is wearing white clothes and safety hospital apparel. A woman gives him a face mask. The two enter the room from where the screams echo. The door shuts behind them, slightly muffling the chilling scream.

Korin stands, frozen in fear, and hears deafening silence.

Korin waits for anything—the man, or another scream—but nothing happens. He walks towards the room and hears a faint cry as he reaches the door. A nurse comes out and looks at him in puzzlement, but she smiles to see his concern. Korin does not hear what she says; he is focused on the sound of a cry. He glimpses at the woman from Rome. She has baggy eyes but smiles at her crying newborn in her arms. A new world in life. Korin recognizes the man, too, who is staring by her side at the little bundle of joy, before the door closes.

"I apologize, but you should be in bed now."

The nurse steps back in surprise at the sight of his grin. "The year is 1960," he says. The nurse nods her head and looks at him with confusion as his lips widen further.

Korin plummets with pain streaming throughout his head. He bites his tongue to alleviate his ache with focus on a lesser pain as he crawls towards the corner to hide from the woman from Rome. He does not want his presence to confuse her. The nurse calls for help, and two more nurses arrive.

"Please, go back. Focus on the baby, not me," he whimpers, but they keep to him. He struggles to get up, buckles to the floor, and soon finds himself thinking without pain. He pleads to the nurses to leave him and leans on the wall to stand up. "It is only a headache, now please prioritize and be with the baby."

The nurse who first saw Korin nods to the other two nurses, who leave to attend to the crying baby. "I am Nurse June," she says.

"Korin Hugo."

"Thank you for your concern, Mr. Hugo. The baby and his mother are fine. There are more than enough nurses helping because there is not much else happening at the moment. How are you, though? You looked ghostly for a moment, and suddenly you seem fine."

"I am not sure, but it's gone now."

The two walk down the corridors with their footsteps echoing across the hall.

"Mr. Hugo, are you lost? I found you lying in front of the hospital door this evening."

"Really?"

"Yes. Do you remember anything?"

"Yes, I just don't remember being in front of a hospital."

She eyes him with suspicions. "Are you some crazy fan?"

"Pardon?"

"Did you know who that couple is?"

"Should I?"

"No, and we'll keep that a secret. Tonight we will shelter you. Tomorrow, I shall check on your headache, but for now, please rest."

"Have you checked upon my condition already?"

"Just the basics. I don't think your headache will be problematic, but I don't understand why you would have one. I didn't find anything unordinary in your data. How frequent is it?"

"It happened twice in the past...it's a bit complicated, but I would say for me it's been two days. It happens when I wake up, but it soon fades away as if nothing happened."

"Yes, well, people do get headaches when they wake up from long or short sleeps, and possibly from sleeping outside in the cold."

They reach the open room, and the nurse bids him farewell. He listens for her footsteps to fade away back the way they came. He looks at the clock in his room. 12:22 AM. Korin plans how to talk to the woman without anyone seeing him let her know that he did not abandon her nine years ago. He ponders if he is traveling through time or having a lucid dream. He observes the clock and returns to planning a way to talk to the woman before the nurse returns, questions his identity, and possibly causes a mess. He wanders to the mirror and looks at his reflection. He is just as young as when he had met her yesterday, or nine years ago. He pokes his face, possibly his proof that he can time travel, and realizes he might have all the time in the world.

He lies in bed and reflects. Back at his childhood park, he wished he was away, slept, and then met the woman at the bench in Rome. In her home, he wished he could see her smile at her newborn, slept, and then observed what he had wished. Wishes. He had wished in the past with great fervor to little avail, so he concludes that something else was responsible for his dream or journey through time. He decides to first test the idea of wishing by repeating in his mind where he wants to go; his subconscious mind would pick up his desires and possibly fulfill them through time travel or a dream. He repeats the thought: "Go to sleep. I want to see her and her infant child in her home." After repeating this thirty times, he lulls to sleep.

"How?"

Korin awakens in a king size bed and looks up at the startled countenance of the woman from Rome. He is cringing, biting his tongue, and, to her amazement, staring wildly through her at nothing.

Korin looks in darkness. His head aches, but he does not know why. He briefly saw the woman's eyes stare at him in shock, but now he feels as though he is falling to nothing, with everything behind him again. Nothing. There is nothing down in the dark depths of an endless ocean.

He cannot cry. He is free of everything, trapped in nothing, sinking to hell.

Korin observes his past as he sinks. He remembers how she calls him Wall-E, like the robot in love with Eve. He thinks of a nickname for her, but stops at the word "Muse," which originally guides one to success. He decides to flip the word and call her Esum, for she was like a Muse taking him deeper into loneliness. He wonders what good is knowing the truth if it does not help prevent problems. Esum did not care if he was older and talked to him first, but when her friends discovered this, they criticized her. He left so that they would stop harassing her. He sees that knowledge brought more awareness of conflict and wishes they were oblivious to their age difference, for all that came of that knowledge was the world's hatred. He knows it is inevitable that they find out each other's age, and he did not want to lie, yet the pain of losing her makes him question the fruitfulness of knowledge. He wonders if his pain, one from trying only to fail with little avail, could be worse than the pain of never knowing what could have been if he acted differently. He hurts because he acted, yet he knows he would still try to help her fight loneliness. That is why he chased her. He saw pain in her eyes and wanted to help her, but now he wallows in pain. He wonders if he should not have chased her.

Loneliness. He sinks in it, describing it as a feeling in which one fully submerges oneself into utter pain caused by reflection of an emotional past. Its strength is determined by the quality and quantity of personal memories. He pauses, thinking there is a better definition.

He does not wish to be alone in this life, so he searches through the many lives for someone to love, needing to love only one girl, yet he experienced the tragedy of being a part of many worlds, of loving the lives of others, raising the kids of others, suffering the pains of others, crying the tears of others, and being torn amongst the many worlds he encountered in others' lives while never being free to live in his own nature. In his quest for love, he found countless lost souls, and his heart reached out to them. They exploited his kindness. He lost his own identity in many worlds for naught. He lost his heart in the hallway. They left him once they received from him what they wanted, left him more broken than he was before. They selfishly progressed towards their futures, abandoning him, with all his labors and aches from aiding them, and ignorantly creating more holes inside him. They were once broken, so he chose to help them recuperate, but they trashed him. They became nothing.

In nature there is one world. In life there are many worlds of people. Korin helped many worlds; in return, they criticized him for loving Esum; their worlds are nothing.

Nonetheless, he hopes. He continues to love others in his quest for Esum because God loved him first. His loneliness thrives. He wholeheartedly aids others and celebrates their successes, but he is still alone, yearning for Esum.

Korin decides: *Loneliness is a desire for something more,*

dissatisfaction with that which is present. Maybe that defines idolization, too.

Korin then sees a light above him. He wonders why this thing returns in his dreams. Korin panics as two blinding lights rush towards him.

"Stop," Korin whimpers. He looks up at the woman across the room, her right hand hovering over a telephone. He remembers where he is and is grateful to hear silence of another kind, with life and light and warmth.

Korin sits up as the woman cautiously stares at him. She sees focus return to his eyes and breathes out. She is still skinny and watches him through kind eyes; although, she is dubious of seeing him. Korin waits for her to gather her thoughts. She has a slightly bigger body after giving birth and seems to have managed fine, her uncanny gratitude constituting to her natural beauty within. He hears silence and wonders where her child is.

"Is your baby asleep?"

She jumps, startled to hear Korin talk, and nods. "You weren't lying then, Korin. You are a time traveler."

"Korin, you were suddenly gone for a few seconds—*physically* gone. One moment you were here, the next moment you disappeared. What happened?"

"I vanished? I'm not sure. This has been happening recently each time after I time travel, or go deeper into my dream."

"Shall I call the hospital?" Her hand is still above the telephone.

"No, thank you. I will be fine."

"You should get that checked."

Korin notices that he is still wearing hospital clothes and explains,

"I was there when you gave birth. I saw you and your husband, and now I am here because I wished to see you and your child in private."

"My husband is working. He'll be back around six this evening." It is 11:07 AM. "Are you still sixteen years old, Korin?"

"Yes, but technically, I am not even born yet."

Korin gets out of bed and converses with her about his hospital visit as she smiles in recollection. She then tells him how young she felt at night in the party, looking at his irrepressible delight in learning to dance with her, and how the memory comforts her. She recalls how she awoke to silence three hours after falling asleep, how she felt an unprecedented emptiness in her apartment, with the gravity of darkness echoing loneliness throughout the area as she hoped she would open her bedroom door to find Korin asleep on the floor, or awake in pensive thought as his eyes often seemed to appear, observing without the impression of protruding. She could get lost in his gaze that seemed to glare at the world due to his arched eyebrows, but she tried to imagine his eyes without eyebrows. They seemed lifeless, yet she saw immense sentiments burning inside them, lighting up the world when released as she noticed when he danced with her. She prayed that the door would reveal to her the truth of seeing Korin in her life, fearing that he was just someone imagined. She hoped in the light she sensed inside him, liberating her of past regrets endured in the cruel reality outside. She edged towards the door. Almost caressing the cold metal knob with her right hand, she slowly pulled the door closer to her chest, which beat with each second until it skipped. "I searched for you in the apartment," she says. "Then the sunlight entered through the blinds, and I saw your shoes. For a moment, I was elated to find proof that you were real, but somehow I felt cold. I sensed that you were gone and realized that

I am going to die before you are born. We cannot coexist, but that night was a miracle. Today is another miracle."

She looks at her friend through tears; she had not felt so isolated in a room since her childhood. Korin is alarmed but remains silent. She sees a mess in his eyes, a woman nine years older since she last saw herself in his gaze. Then she realizes he is staring at her with his mouth curved in worry. He still looks inside of her, the same way he had looked at her in 1951. He did not change. He is the same friend she found on the bench. He still cares for her and so has returned. He had not left her on purpose as he just explained to her but had actually time traveled to see her smile at her child. Despite her joy, tears stream down as she struggles to control her breathing. He came back for her in private, just as they were in Rome.

Korin shifts in panic at her tears. *Did I do something wrong?*

"Sorry, Korin."

"You remember my name," he remarks.

"Of course I do."

"Am I still part of your happiest memory in life?"

"One of the happiest moments in my life."

Korin sighs in relief. "I hoped that your marriage and child would constitute the better memories in your life."

"Yes, but I will not forget you." She wipes away her tears and laughs. "I really shouldn't be crying. I don't mean to depress you."

"I didn't mean to make you cry."

"I made myself cry. Silly me."

"We're in Switzerland?"

"Yes, how did you know?"

"I read a book about you in my time."

"What did it say about me?"

"You are one of a kind..."

"Oh, that's too much."

"...and modest."

They walk down the stairs as they speak and then sit in the living room where she decides to bring tea. She needs tea to assuage herself, unaware that her excitement elicits the same slight jumps in her steps of the night they met. As she heats the kettle, she remarks, "I don't think I know much about you."

"What would you like to know?"

"Where are your parents?"

"They should be at my apartment at night in the future."

"Did you run away that night I found you?"

"Yes." He explains what happened in the events leading up to his departure to his childhood park. "I slept on a bench and subconsciously wished I could be with you, and then you woke me up."

"So if I tell myself to go to the future to you, will you wake me up?"

"I do not think so. I've made wishes before, but that was the first time mine came true through time travel or a dream."

"What did you wish for before?"

"I wanted a girlfriend, which to me was someone I could talk to and laugh with. She would be kind, smart, and preferably pretty; although, that last one isn't necessary."

"How old were you?" she marvels.

"I was about five years old in the first grade."

She laughs. "How did your girlfriend turn out?"

"I don't have one. I found a friend in *HER*. She tapped my hand first and told me to chase her when I didn't know who she was, and from then on we fell in love. She left me, though. She is younger than me, and eventually her friends got her to think that she couldn't be with me because of the difference in age."

"Let's give your friend a nickname so that I won't be confused. I think it is strange to address your friend as *HER* with such emphasis, almost as if she is a goddess."

"Oh, that was not my intention," he says in shock.

"I know," she smiles comfortingly, "but that makes it all the more prevalent," she adds with a calm gaze. "You don't realize how much you idolize her."

"I don't want her name to be common, not that common names are terrible. I want something that has to do with one." He pauses. "Esum!" he recalls. "It is muse, but backwards."

"Well, compared to you, how much younger is Esum?"

"Seven years and eighty-nine days."

The kettle boils. The woman walks to the kitchen, sets up cups, and recoils when she spills hot tea on the table. She did not expect Korin to love a nine-year old girl. She decides she can only handle one cup with her shaking hands and so takes it to Korin.

Open

The two converse while lying opposite each other on separate chairs, a small table in between them where the kettle is. The warm tea soothes their bodies and alleviates their worries, while their words relieve them of unwanted loneliness.

A silence ensues. Korin looks down at the dark liquid swirling in his cup, steam rising with a pleasing aroma and condensing at his chin.

"I'm sorry we can't go outside. I know you feel uncomfortable with being alone with a woman."

"That's okay. Now that you're famous, the paparazzi would make a mess if they saw us and I suddenly disappeared. I guess technically we're not alone even though your son is asleep and he's too young to make sense of us, but we can leave the windows open so that you can scream for help if anything bad happens."

"Oh, Korin, I trust you."

Korin observes the young boy's breathing in a crib as he gently asks, "Do you mind telling me about your childhood? It's okay if you don't want to."

"That's all right. I was born in Belgium, 1929, and raised in the Netherlands during World War II. I grew up hungry, so I would read sometimes to keep my mind elsewhere and at least feed my imagination. We managed to escape with my grandmother, who cleverly changed my name on my papers so that the Germans would not discover my British ethnicity, which, at the time, was a disadvantage. I originally wanted to be a dancer, but my teacher told me that I was too tall to become a professional. Since then, I never quite liked the way I looked. My nose is too big, and I'm so skinny and freakishly tall that I stand out like a sore thumb among beautiful Hollywood stars. They have such big, authentic auras compared to little me. I do appreciate my fortune, though. I've had so much fun with all my movies, even the ones that weren't so popular. I've met wonderful people who have guided me through this business, and I met my husband in a film we worked on, but you probably know the rest from that biography you read.

"I must say it is a bit disconcerting to think that my life will be described by some stranger in a numbered amount of pages. I like to think that there is more to life, but I also like to think it is simple. I had to work very hard to get to where I am, but I have to thank those people who have helped me during the war. UNICEF was particularly important to me at that time, giving me food and books so that I came out all right. I would like to work for them in the future, but first I shall take care of my child. If only I had three children, without the two miscarriages, but right now I am overjoyed with one. My beautiful Sean. I have a husband who I work with occasionally and a child to love. I have a family, and that's all I truly want. Remember? We talked about that in my apartment. Although you might know most of this already if you have read about me."

"Yes, but your personal tone births new meaning to cold facts. It's as if your voice brings hearty authenticity that makes me believe and so understand what has happened at a higher capacity than that from reading about it."

"What…," she says dubiously, while Korin respectfully waits in silence. "What…do you know about me?"

"All that you just said and some other information, such as the films you will star in."

She gazes at him, simultaneously enchanted and perturbed with Korin's admiration for her and the potential of knowing her future.

"How about…. Should I ask about my future? I could maybe prevent mistakes."

"You should accept what you have now. You don't need to know about what will happen until that time comes."

She looks at the ground as Korin watches her come to terms with herself. "Well, I agree," she says, smiling. "What should we do now? We must stay in the house, though, unless I carry Sean outside, but I would like to keep him asleep without disturbing him. Actually, what's your favorite song?"

"I don't really have one, but I would like to make a song that talks about the trinity." She eagerly asks him to sing it for her, so he nervously sings, "'I want to be with you, God of the universe,'" elders and youths declare in all of their eulogies (x2).

"I want to be with you (x3). Jesus, I want to be with you.

"I want to be with you (x2). Jesus, I want to be with you.

"Over creation above and below, you are Lord of everything. Oh, Father God, Christ the Son of God and Man, and Holy Spirit are three in one. Yes, he's omnipotent, omniscient, omnipresent, and transcendent in wisdom and holiness. Gracious and faithful, immutable, just in His wrath with infinite goodness. He's merciful, eternal, self-sufficient and self-existent. He's triune with divine love. I will sing with the church and trust in the Bible, your Word. Angels rejoice above. Rejoice in Christ in all circumstances. Remember His Word and His self-sufficiency.

"Together we sing (x2). Jesus, you are with me."

The woman, who was grinning as he sang, quietly yet enthusiastically applauds so as not to wake up Sean. Korin blushes and thanks her for her kindness as they continue to enjoy their conversation.

A sound comes from the door, and Korin gets between the woman and the door to protect her from a potential intruder. He sees the door unlock and realizes that her husband might have come home early, so he runs up the stairs. The woman quickly takes his cup and hides it in the sink just as the door opens. Her husband barges in.

"Henry, is everything all right?" she says slightly loud enough to assure Korin upstairs that there is no intruder.

She looks around for Korin, for she does not want to risk her husband's anger at seeing her with a boy or explain time traveling.

"The plans for production are outrageous!"

"Henry, the baby is asleep."

"Right, sorry. I wish I could fall asleep like him without a care in the world. The studio won't give me a proper budget."

"I'm sure you can work something out."

"That's easy for you to say with your charm. Everybody loves you. You don't understand what it means to be a man in this business, fighting everyone who comes your way just so you can get the picture moving."

"That's not right of you to say."

"Life isn't right. The whole world is wrong."

"We should be thankful for what we have."

"Yes, of course," he says as he takes off his jacket and enters the living room. "Give me some tea. That's just what I needed." She does so. He growls, "It's not hot enough. Nothing is the way it should be."

"You always want more."

"Of course. I can always do better; I can always accomplish my best, only there is no best achievement, so I keep aspiring for satisfaction in a moment, knowing well enough that I will never be satisfied, but I abhor a second-class result and so I keep trying to improve."

They walk up the stairs as Korin hears their voices from the closet room of the master bedroom. He curses himself for going to that room, but his legs naturally took him to the room where he had awakened.

"Why don't you take a break?" she asks as they enter the room. "We have more than enough money."

"How can you decline potential success when the chance calls to you?"

"Will you keep your voice down for Sean, please?"

"You don't tell me what to do. You should be the proper woman of the house instead of gaining all the popularity you want, while I actually work for a living."

"I work, too. You shouldn't be jealous of me; you have a nice career." She quickly searches for any sign of Korin as Henry walks towards the closet.

Henry opens the door but rapidly turns to her and says, "I will continue to reach the front as far as I can go until I am buried under the unprecedented line I establish for my legacy."

"Is that what life is about?"

"Life is about controlling the world around you."

"What am I to you?"

"That's for you to decide."

"I would rather be kind and quickly forgotten by this world than rude and remembered."

"Rude?"

"This isn't like you. You have been kind to me, and I to you, but suddenly you're so different. I love you for who you are, and popularity has nothing to do with us."

"That's easy for you to say with your fame."

"I was alone for the longest time of my life, including during the war. Fame is the last thing on my mind. All I want is to love God and a family in you and our child."

Henry pauses and looks away in guilt. "Then leave."

"Why?"

"Leave! I'm moving on."

"How can you abandon your family that loves you?"

"Why not?"

"Look for what is right in the family. If you keep doing things and asking, 'Why not?' that means your heart is looking for an excuse to do what you know is wrong and reassert what you already believe in. You're not living to learn what is right; you're living to find anything that confirms what you think is right. I can understand you leaving if you are following God's command, and, though I may not like it, I would believe that He is leading you to the right direction, but that is not the case. Even if the family is cruel to you, you should forgive and love them, but I haven't been cruel to you. Henry, I love you."

"Don't talk back to me!" Henry punches the closet door and leaves. "I'm going out!"

Korin heaves a sigh of relief as he hears Henry stomp away, but fury soon overwhelms him. He remains patient, though, knowing that his sudden appearance would not help. The front door slams as Korin sighs. This is their affair to suture.

She falls to the floor in tears, failing to hide from nature and life, trapped in society. Korin slowly walks out, thankful that the noise had not awakened Sean. He sits against the dented closet door, hurting as he hears her muffled sobs.

No one hears her cries except him, yet he can do nothing without altering time and life. He looks up at the dent before closing his eyes, focusing on the pain of the world.

Korin shivers. He brings his knees near his body, but the cold burns. He opens his eyes and looks up at the dark sky. Korin jumps up to a sitting position. An unholy stench of fire overwhelms the grey debris amidst a cloud of ash that pitifully gasps for its mutant existence. Crumbling rocks groan beneath Korin's bare feet, breaking an artificial silence as he stands in the middle of a deserted street. A deafening boom shakes the earth, and Korin instinctively drops with his hands over his head. His ears ring as he looks behind him. Smoke shrouds tall buildings that had once held life but are now shattered. Pain pierces his mind, unable to think as he agonizes with increasing intensity for a minute. His whole body involuntarily shakes as he lies otherwise in paralysis so that he cannot will himself to bite his tongue to distract his mind with another kind of pain. A second explosion booms even closer, deafening him as his heart screams. He remains motionless, unable to see the brooding sky above the swarm of dust. He barely feels something lift him and take him down as a person closes a cellar door behind him, bringing in darkness. Korin senses other presences nearby, but he faints, while the earth crunches under the bombs of vanity.

A little girl grasps her mother's ragged clothes from behind as they observe the stranger on the floor. The explosions ceased about an hour ago, but no one dares to speak a word. The little girl barely makes out the dark figure whose face she had barely seen when her father brought him in, but suddenly she cannot see him. She looks at her mother's figure, and then at the spot where the boy was. He vanished.

Korin hears crying and opens his eyes to light. The woman's voice soothes her child, a little world embraced warmly in her arms. Korin's mind hurts again, and he closes the closet to return to darkness. He needs to live in the truth, in darkness with the world, for he, a witness to the horrors of Man's wars against nature, refuses to see life through light. The light is an insult to the darkness that had shrouded the war. His tears rush down his face, but he does not want to disturb the woman and Sean, so he keeps the door closed. He feels a gentle push from the outside. Korin desperately hides, but darkness betrays him as light penetrates the space, leaving him helplessly exposed. He turns away to cower in his shadow. The world is vain, for no one hears its perpetual cries.

There seems to be light, but the inevitable night reigns truth upon Man's hopelessness. Korin looks up at the dented door. Nothing had changed since his time travel to World War II. Henry is still blinded by power, the woman and her child are crying when no one will help, and the door fails to withstand oppression, to do its duty of keeping out the unwanted and keeping in the wanted. All pain of every life barges into Korin's mind as he begs to be relieved of this false light. He wants to hide alone in darkness, the true atmosphere of life. Before God made the world, there was darkness, and so there should be now.

"Korin?" a gentle voice whispers. "Korin, may I come in?"

Korin anticipates pain and pity in her face, but she is smiling. She wants to join him in the darkness but does not intrude. She opened the door enough so that her expression was just visible, her silhouette covering most of the light outside. The woman's voice reminds him of life itself: a sweet, kind tone of hope in love.

"You don't have to ask. This is your closet after all," he says as his headache fades away.

"All right then. I think Sean should meet you. Don't you, Sean?" she whispers to the baby who curiously looks up at her. "I'll sit in my closet if you don't mind then."

Korin looks at her as she sits and leaves the door slightly open. He looks at the baby who marvels at him with the big, clean, pure whites around his brown pupils, full of new life and curiosity. Korin smiles, and Sean awkwardly imitates the motion. Korin laughs, and Sean hysterically responds alike, and the three laugh together.

She opens the door and lets Sean crawl about, while she beckons to Korin to join her outside the closet. She sees Korin wipe away his tears with a grin, but he flinches and glares around him. He raises his hand for silence, as if hearing something she cannot. Korin lies on his side, his right ear pressing against the wooden floor. She shivers as Korin suddenly plops on his back, his eyes plain and unseeing. A strange familiarity lurks in her mind, as though she had seen Korin in the darkness before when she was little. She feels her skin warm, as if an invisible being breathes farewell upon her, its spiritual, burning cold presence having filled the room with sudden intensity before its sudden absence is felt in a revived surge of warmth. She searches for Sean and finds him by the bed staring at the closet. She turns around. Korin vanished.

Infinite

Darkness, a dense aura in endless space that reeks of the pure death of souls apart from rotting flesh, envelops Korin in putrid horror, echoing pitiful silent screams. Korin stands and walks around with his hand reaching for a nonexistent closet wall. He struggles with each step as though trudging through a stagnant pool. He plunges into lukewarm liquid-like substance, unable to float or swim, yet able to breathe. He sinks. A light shines in the distance above him, and Korin reaches for it, uncertain as to why he should yet certain that he must. Then he realizes that there are two lights close to each other, but his brain cries in agony that renders him unconscious.

Korin feels warm, hard ground, his head now serene. He touches peculiar lines that seem to form a pattern, but he cannot see. He looks forward and sees the two sources of light pointing ahead of him. They appear to be connected to the ground Korin is on when he hears the slight sound of liquid parting. He is on something that is sailing or swimming across a body of unknown, transparent liquid, something with lights illuminating darkness, revealing nothing.

Then, the liquid turns brown like dark blood. Korin feels the traces of a dying wave bump against the object beneath him. The ground beneath him lurches to a stop, and the lights close to pitch blackness. After a few minutes, the most peculiar cry resonates around him as Korin feels the ground shaking beneath him. His ears echo the cry of horror even after it is done, yet Korin feels a revelation. It is the sound that he had been looking for, the cry that finally compounds anger, pain, and sorrow—all their heartfelt veracities—into a masterful cry. At last, he is truly in the dark. He feels renewed, his brain relieved of the psychological barrier that society instilled in him, of holding in his feelings, the cry having done justice in transmitting his emotions unto sound, thereby freeing them and loosening his brain from pent up frustration. He grins, but feels tears stream down his face as a new sadness overtakes him in sympathy towards the cry. He wonders where it came from, but he is still lost, still trapped wherever he is in his dream or time travels, still searching for truth with his mind—his troubled, troubled mind.

The ground moves on, but the light remains gone. Korin lies down and attempts to fall asleep as he thinks to himself to awaken at his childhood park. All he knows is that he must go back to the hallway and retrieve his heart for his hollow chest. He tells himself that everything he had seen so far was just a convoluted dream. He decides to awaken back at the park. He still wonders if he is a time traveler, however, so he thinks about returning to the school hallway. He falls asleep.

Korin awakens and sees darkness. He looks around him and sees two white lights shining on calm, transparent liquid.

"How do I get out of here?" he calls out in vain. Korin sees something in the distance. It grows larger, and Korin realizes that he is on something that is sailing or swimming at an alarming rate despite the smooth ride Korin is having. He gapes at the now large sphere, only seven stories above them, but it is falling. Earth is falling.

"My name is Salvador. I am the salvation of my world and yours. I am the one who gave you the power to time travel."

Korin feels the ground shake beneath him, his heart leaping from the sudden bass-baritone voice.

"Where are you?"

"I am beneath you. You are standing on my shell."

Korin's voice cracks, so he coughs and says, "You said you give me power."

"I am the reason why you can time travel. I instilled in your mind the ability to time travel through your dreams when you were an infant."

"I'm dreaming."

"You are not. You are a time traveler. You are in The Time Realm, the body of liquid Time connecting the galaxy."

"Time can't be a liquid."

"It is. It is not like what your people call liquid, such as water, which is why you can breathe in liquid Time. You can sink in it; you can let it choke you; or you can breathe in it."

"What are you?"

"My kind resembles what your people call tortoises, but we are far more intelligent than them and much larger in size. You dreamt of me once. Remember?"

Korin recalls the ancient ruins and how he saw the giant tortoise.

"I am the last of my kind, but my companions are not dead. Their memories are implanted in my mind so that they live on inside of me. Korin, you are going to help me use your planet to save my kind. In three hours, in terms of time here in the Time Realm, my planet will die."

"Why didn't you ask me earlier? What am I even talking about?

How can I possibly help you save your kind if they're just memories?" Korin asks.

"I will answer your questions, but first we must make haste," Salvador says coolly. "You must make a choice. You are different from the rest of your people. You stand out, and I have seen your dreams. You are alone, but you are kind. You, Korin, are the only one I can trust."

"There are plenty of kind people who are alone. I'm no different from them."

"I chose you, and God chose you, and the Devil chose to tempt you into sin because he fears your love. Most people in your world do not even have love."

"Don't all the couples in the world have love?"

"Some of them do, but most of them are living lies. Most of your people love selectively, but true love loves all. You, however, are alone, just as Christ did not have a female lover. You are chosen by God, so I will not kill you lest God harm me. Your choice is to either commit suicide or choose one other person to live with on Earth before I wipe out everyone else's memories."

"Why would God choose me? I pushed my mother, and I have done many sins you do not know."

"I do not know the specifics, but God chooses the weak to lead the strong. The Holy Spirit entered many sinners, and they became workers of righteousness. Now you are chosen."

"Why would I kill myself?"

"I have no authority to kill you, but I am going to wipe out the memories of everyone else. Then, I will fill their minds with the memories of my kind. You will be the only true human left, and if that thought depresses you, you can kill yourself. Otherwise, you can choose to have one person live with you. I have too many memories in my mind. Even with the entire human race, I would still have to sacrifice some memories of my kind. Still, I know the pain of being the last of one's kind, so I offer you your choice of one companion."

"You can erase memories?"

"Yes. My kind has studied time travel for eons and has discovered that it involves memories and dreams. A fellow worker and I have discovered the ability to time travel through space, or send our Spirits to other worlds and explore the minds of inhabitants through dreams. Every planet we have reached out to has been biologically inferior, leaving us with no foundation to colonize the planet and survive. There is one other planet, however, that we tried to contact. The inhabitants of that planet refused us, so we respected their wish. We knew that our planet would burn up in our star, so we continued to search for a new suitable home. We finally reached your planet, the best option so far, but your people have obstinate minds.

"Time travel is an inherent ability that your people forget quickly but not completely. That is why dreams exist. Dreams are the remaining bits of time travel, and those who often remember their dreams are more likely to time travel. Only two of your people have been able to time travel because you are all ignorant fools. You all forget your dreams and time traveling powers. You swine take such pearls for granted.

"My kind had been contacting your people for centuries, but only a select few have responded. After reaching out to several men and women, we finally managed to send a man back in time, but the conceited human was too rash and nearly altered your timeline, so we sent him back to his time and erased those parts of his memories. Then, my kind saw the horrors your people commit in murders and were convinced that we could not reason with your people, knowledgeable monsters, so we decided to erase your memories, but God spoke to us through dreams, saying that there is an Observer who we cannot kill. I found you.

"To answer why it took me so long to speak to you, I am light years away from your planet and so had difficulty telepathically speaking to you with my Spirit. It's a miracle enough that I could send my Spirit into your world and bring you to the Time Realm with about three hours to spare. Here in the Time Realm, my Spirit can reside in my body and you in yours. Here there are representations of the planets, but all is dark because that is how everything was when there was only God. There are no stars or moons here, for my kind is not yet capable of creating them here. In other words, my kind are Creators of the Time Realm, like God is of everything, yet my kind's Time Realm is still inferior in representing all of God's creations. Here as well as in my world, time is much slower than it is on Earth. Three hours in my world and the Time Realm is thirty minutes in yours."

"You plan to kill the human race other than me and another person of my choice."

"Not quite. God might save some of your people who are righteous."

"But you're going to take over Earth."

"I like to think that I am saving it. Your people are killing Earth."

"What happened to the rest of your kind?"

"My kind has flaws, too. With the discovery of time travel, evil intent and temptation brought about war for the power of time travel, and they killed each other or ended their lives."

"Why can't you just travel back in time and prevent all of that?"

"Why don't you go back in time to stop a catastrophe? You are afraid of changing the timeline. I share the same fear."

"But you are trying to save your kind."

"I will not play God. To do so without God's blessing is beyond foolish, so the situation will only get worse."

"Aren't you playing God by creating the Time Realm?"

"I am creating a representation of God's creations, much like your artists do."

"What about killing God's people?"

"I am doing what your people have done to each other in their conquests."

"How does that make you any better if you are killing for what you want like people did?"

"I am doing this to save your world and my kind. Your people want more land, more of anything to fill their hearts with imperfect things of this world. They kill to get what they want. They want everything. I am not like that. I want the happiness of my kind. I am better than your people because I am filled with love for my people and God. I am trying to save my kind. When Christ died on the cross, he said, 'It is finished.' He set up the foundation for us to do good works in his absence, and now he lives in heaven, blessed on the right-hand throne beside God as reward for his sacrifice. Your people have had their chances to do good, yet I see too much pain in your world. That is why it is time for your people to rest forever. I will erase their memories and let them die peacefully. Then, my kind will inhabit their minds and be saved while your people are sent, according to God's judgment, to heaven or hell."

"Who are you to judge who should die?"

"I have seen your judges. I have seen their corrupt bargains. I have seen the lives of your people perish by the horrors they inflict upon each other, and I have decided to end all their miseries. Earth will be home to my kind. My planet, Kra, will be like the one we passed by."

"I don't know what planet you're referring to. Was I asleep?"

"If you were, I probably woke you up with my cry." Korin remembers the beautiful cry of mourning. "We passed by what was left of a small planet on the way here. The planet died soon after I brought you to the Time Realm, and many souls cried out as they descended to hell. The blood of their souls floated in liquid Time until it thinned out to transparent oblivion."

"Korin, I understand that your options are difficult to appreciate, so I will let you time travel to your world for twenty minutes in terms of Earth's time. For me in the Time Realm, that is two hours. That leaves me about half an hour in the Time Realm when you return, more than enough time to erase everyone's mind when you return."

"Will you take me to the time when Jesus did his first miracle?"

"God specifically forbid me from taking you to Jesus' time because Jesus will not be there. Jesus is in heaven. Even if I tried, I could only take you to a time after Jesus' twelve disciples have all died."

Korin looks up at the world above him. "Man of the world. I will be responsible for the fate of the world. I don't want to be the man of the world. It's lonely to be here, with holes through my chest from the wounds of the world's wars. I saw the horrors of war when I accidentally time traveled to World War II when I looked at the hole Henry made on the closet door and thought about the woman's childhood. I just want to help people, while God does the saving, but how can I if I can only choose one? How can I help everyone with so much hurting? Why can't I help them all? Why do I have to sacrifice anyone? Why do I have to choose who lives? Why does my flesh do what my spirit does not want?

"I want everyone to be loved. Everyone. No one should have to go through the loneliness I felt when I was four. But these holes hurt so much that I can't concentrate anymore. I don't even know what matters anymore if everyone will die. What kind of world is this where so much fear and pain get the better of so many potential leaders of God? I don't believe in heroes; I believe in leaders, but the way things are, there will only be hatred and sadness so that the ideas of heroes and leaders become myths. Let me be that myth, at least as the last one, by letting my people live. I don't know how I can help you. I want you to live, too."

"Why would you want to save them? What does it matter if your people will not love you? They will all die eventually."

"I don't know. I just know I have to try. I always have."

"They left you alone because they were ignorant. They don't care about anyone but themselves."

"I'll die trying to help my people. I love them."

"But they do not love you. I don't understand you."

"I love the world despite the holes it puts in my heart because God loved me first."

"I will acknowledge that your words are honorable, and I have seen parts of your life from a distance up to now. I can see why you are the chosen one, for you are truly kind and loving, but you cannot do anything to stop me. Now, have you made up your mind, Korin? I suggest you time travel now."

"Yes, take me to Africa."

"You can do that yourself Korin. I gave you the power through your dream of me. Your head will hurt each time you time travel because you are taking all of your memories and transporting them with you. At first, it did not hurt you because the power I gave you was still strong. With each time travel, your power weakened and caused you pain. I will restore that power so that you do not suffer a headache. I will bring you back here when it is time."

"What will you do while you wait?"

"I'll reflect on the countless memories I have."

"I understand."

Korin hears a gasp. After a moment of shock, the wrinkled woman whispers, "Korin, who's dreaming this time? You or me?"

He laughs but stops. "You are beautiful as always."

"Oh stop it. I just wish I had a heads up of when you would come back. I'm so terribly sorry for the mess. If only you had returned sooner.... I knew you weren't just some dream, but when you were gone for several decades, I doubted that I would see you again, yet here you are. You are such a handsome young man. How old are you again? Oh, that doesn't matter. I am a bit embarrassed that you are still young, whereas my body is riddled with wrinkles and old age."

"You are very beautiful. In fact, you look even more beautiful now," he says truly. "You don't need to worry about your appearance or the room. Everyone grows old, and I don't know what you're talking about for the room. It looks fine." He looks at the woman in bed. There is medicine on a table beside her, yet her smile and tears give no sign of illness.

"I'm sorry," she says, wiping her tears. "I'm just so glad."

"I'm sorry that I made you wait. It was selfish of me."

She ponders for a minute before she says, "It was—"

"I should've—"

"—worth it. I don't regret meeting you for a second. I knew

what I was because you told me, so it's not selfish of you. I wanted to spend time with you, so I joined you, and I would not have had it any other way."

Korin struggles to smile with his heavy heart. "I wish I could do something grand. Something beyond fantastic," he says as his eyes water. "Something beyond the 'beyond,' and even beyond that 'beyond the beyond.' I love you, my dear friend. I love you so much that I hurt because I know the problems you will face yet am helpless to resolve them for the sake of preserving the way life is without time travel." A sinking sensation clouds his innards, like a storm raging in his chest. "Time is running out. I just wish I knew how to better describe what I wish. This 'beyond the beyond the beyond.'" Tears stream down his face. "Something that cannot be imagined within the scope of a mortal mind. Then, I understand that God's love is what I want for you. He is beyond the infinite beyond." Korin chokes out the last sentence as he involuntarily shakes with sorrow. "I wish... that I could give you...all the love that He has."

"You already have."

"But I can always do more for you."

"You already have. Thank you. Do not worry, my dear friend. I believe that God has used you to introduce His love for me. For that, you already have given me the infinite beyond. You gave me the news of God, and I fell in love with that. Thank you. Truly."

The storm inside Korin fills up his chest with rain. "No, I was selfish. I initially wanted to see you to ask you why and how you have such an optimistic perspective of the world. You lived through the second world war." He does not want to remind her of her painful past, but he has no time. He must be direct. "You lost your father three times. He moved away when you were a child. As an adult, you found him and tried to bond with him, but he was unsure of how to react. He was complacent, and your heart broke even further. The third time, you lost him forever." Korin heaves as he struggles to breathe through his tears. "You said that you did not view him as your father, but rather as someone you wanted to care for." He feels himself drowning. "Still, you hurt when he did not respond as you had hoped he would. Now you still long for the father's love, but you cannot find it." Korin's heart is gasping for air above the ocean in his chest. "You had relationships, including two marriages that you were loyal to." His eyes are leaking pure streams of fat liquid anger. "Still, your husbands were cruel to you. They left. The biography I read quotes your words that you cannot hate them because they were kind people, but you are lying." His chest starts shaking as Korin hyperventilates, but he pounds his chest. His tears inside flood his chest, but he wills himself to focus. "You are too kind to truly hate anyone. You lied because you do not want people to hate your former husbands and so ruin their careers as actors." His heart sinks in the body of water. "You lied to protect them when they abandoned you. How can you do that?" He drops to his knees beside her bed and pants painfully. "After all of your pains, how is it that you still love people so much?"

"Korin, is something else bothering you?"

"The world.... End. Salva.... I...choose...."

"Korin, I don't understand what you're saying. You need to calm down. Stand up and put your hands over your head." Korin feels her soft hands reach him again. He gets up so that she does not strain herself to pick him up, but she is just three inches from his face and looking deep into his eyes. "Korin, you're going to be all right. Breathe in." She pauses as Korin obeys. "Breathe out." She helps him sit on her bed as he controls his breathing. "It's okay to let your emotions out, but you've got to watch your breathing, Korin." She kisses him on the forehead and holds him in a surprisingly strong yet soothing embrace. She quickly lets go so that he can breathe again. Korin blinks away his tears and looks up at her. She looks blurry through his tears, and he smiles.

"I am reminded of the time we first met at the bench," he says. "I couldn't see you well as my eyes adjusted to the light, but I could hear your kind voice asking if I was all right. Do you remember?"

She smiles and hands him a jujube.

She respectfully stands as Korin recovers in a minute. He gets up and asks her to sit down, realizing that he had taken her spot on the bed. Instead, she makes him stay as she sits beside him.

"What were you saying about the world?"

"The world is ending. Basically, the reason why I can time travel is because another creature gave me the power. It is from another planet and has the appearance resembling a gigantic tortoise. He gave me the choice of saving one person from my timeline to live with me while everyone else loses their memories. I have less than twenty minutes before it all happens."

"My goodness. Why did you visit me?" she asks, but she remembers what Korin said earlier. "Oh, yes. You said I am optimistic and that you want to understand. Well, I think of my life in this manner: I am here today by the graces of some wonderful people. There are times when people have hurt me, and my memories of the war terrify me to this day. Still, there is so much to be thankful for, and I don't have time to play around like most people seem to do. I want to help people, and I thank God for reminding me that there is love. I do not always feel happy, but I always have joy in saving God's people. Helping the hungry Africans here has opened up my heart these past years. That is why I am optimistic. I have joy in serving the God who I love so much by serving the least of His people. His love is worth all the pain the world throws at me, so I continue to hope in God. Does that answer your question?"

"Yes, but the world is now about to end. What's the point now? I can't save God's people. They're all going to die."

"You're from the future. I don't like to think of this, but most people of my generation are already dead in your timeline. Having death in mind changes nothing. In some manner, I already knew; everyone knew that they were going to die, but that didn't keep us from living. The point is the same before and after we live, that is, to glorify God and so love people; therefore, I suggest you live life for God right now. Go save as many people as you can through God's righteousness with what little time you have left. Don't ever give up on God."

"This is it, though. I won't selfishly risk changing the timeline by talking with anyone else. This is my last time travel, so you're the last person I can talk to. It's going to end very soon. What do we do?"

She pauses. "Enjoy it." She smiles. "Let's talk until one of us leaves."

"What do we talk about?"

"I wonder. What *does* one talk about before the end of the world?"

"I think I know. Let's say what we think about each other."

"That sounds wonderful. Let's do that."

"I'll start. I'll describe you in third person, though. I think that gives you the idea of seeing yourself from a new perspective, so that might be interesting."

"Okay, whenever you're ready."

"She is a girl of...sorry, how old are you right now?"

"That's all right. I'm sixty-three years old."

"She is a girl of sixty-three years, but that is not the first impression. She first walks to a bench in 1951. This girl, whose name I did not know at the time, walked toward her home until she sees notices a male youth whose presence is conspicuous in an otherwise desolate garden.

"She sees him curled up, as she had done so during the war. Memories of her childhood during World War II return, but she disregards them, for they are of the past. These days, she is in an apartment in Rome, but she is alone. Her father is busy. He is an old man who had left her when she was young, so the years without a father's love have piled onto her so that she had matured while yearning for love. She does all the work herself because she had learned to take responsibility. No one else would deal with her demons.

"There is a sharp pain of frustrating nostalgia within her. She does not join in the worlds' silly little games because she does not have time for them. She has tried to enjoy life, but the reality of life goes against her efforts. As a result, she has a tinge of resentment towards such happiness of others that seems artificial to her whenever she returns to her apartment that does not feel like home. She does not interact with her father because there is no point in doing so now. She feels that her upbringing had his absence for so long that she would be uncomfortable if their relationship changed, so she stays apart and keeps to herself.

"There is a sense of freedom in those rare moments of chosen solitude, but it is also painful. She wants to be alone, but she also wants to be with someone to talk to. There is no one to talk to. She had prayed many times before, but she feels guilty for not knowing more about God and is dubious of His grace in her troubled life.

"She does well to maintain her composure, but she feels such loneliness within.

"That is why she smiles when the youth on the bench stutters. She feels the warmth of what a relationship is when it is held together. Her mother and father divorced when she was a child. Still, she sees people suffering like she is. No one else notices. No one else cares."

She quickly rolls her eyes in agreement.

"She does not want to leave people because they ask her for help. She can help them even though no one is helping her. That is why she greets the stranger on the bench and ascertains of his well-being. She wants to spread kindness in this cursed world.

"She is prepared to leave everything, though. She is going to several countries for her movie. She wants to start her career early at the age of twenty-three, an age that is younger than when most actors star in Hollywood films. She had taken dancing classes she enjoyed, but she is too tall to become a dancer. Meanwhile, she continues to help people; she gives them advice, but she feels that something is lacking in her. She feels guilty for not going to church and feels hypocritical, so she does not talk about God, who she does not feel too close to. Nonetheless, her life is ahead of her. Time is running out, so she works hard to earn money.

"She is independent. She is polite. She is lost. She is intelligent in worldly matters. She is looking for love and understanding, for she does not see that in her family or past churches. She decides to give God another chance, unaware that it is God who is giving her the chance to come meet Him through the youth on the bench. That does not mean that another person is needed to encounter God, for one can grow to love God alone, but she needs encouragement.

"Thank God that she chooses to wake up the youth."

She is smiling. "That was actually very accurate. In fact, there are things that you said that I didn't even know about myself, but when you said it, it made sense. It's like you thought my thoughts out for me. When did you think of all this?"

"Just now."

"Really? Wow," she marvels. "Well, yeah," she says, at a loss for what to say as she looks up in wonder. "That was cool. Yeah...that was cool."

"Was I wrong anywhere?"

"No, no you got it. That's really cool."

"What part were you referring to when you said that I thought out thoughts for you?"

"Well, it was that part about why I smile to see you on the bench. That no one else cares about anything, but that it doesn't discourage me because I still want relationships with people, that I want to help people and spread kindness in this cursed world. Those parts and what you said in between those parts."

"Interesting," Korin says as he pauses. He had been looking at her eyes while he spoke about his thoughts of her, and she had an intelligent look in her eyes. He remembers the same look in her eyes in 1951, how it searched for understanding, gazed with calm assurance and subtle curiosity, yet maintained a gentle quality in its focus, balanced with measured respect, without intrusion, and truly caring for what it sees, as though its subject is of utmost importance. "I hope that helped you in some way," he says, unaware of how useful his words are to her.

"Absolutely. It helped clarify some things that I was wondering about. This is really cool. No one has ever done something like this before for me. It's really cool. Thank you," she says with a genuine smile.

Korin smiles back. "So, what do you think about me, if you don't mind sharing?"

"Not at all. I don't think I'll do a long one like you did. I'll write down words that I think describe you well."

"Okay, cool."

He waits for several minutes and looks around at the room. The walls are light brown and bare. There is one lamp on in the relatively dark room, but it is bright enough to make the room less gloomy. It shines upon Korin and the woman's faces as she ponders what to write. He looks around the floor where clothes are strewn about.

"I'm sorry about the mess. This is how girls tend to 'organize' their space, especially when they don't think a guy is going to time travel to their room," she teases.

"It's okay. I don't mind." He looks at her side of the room to find a single suitcase neatly placed beside her bed. "How long have you been in Africa to help the children?"

"This trip has lasted about two months, but it seems like I will have to return to Switzerland soon. My stomach does not feel too well."

Korin frowns because he knows what will happen to her, but he does not say anything.

"Don't worry, Korin," she says as he sees his reflection in her eyes. "I think I know what I have. I'm not afraid of dying. I mainly want to see my children."

"I understand." He looks at her in silent admiration.

"I'm done," she says after a few more minutes. She hands him a paper. "Don't lose it."

"I promise I will never lose it." Korin reads the paper, and he bursts with laughter after reading the first word.

"Yeah, I thought that word fit you," she laughs. "Am I right, though?" she asks with concern in case she offended him with a misinterpretation.

"No, no. It makes sense," he laughs. "I just didn't expect that to be the first word you would write. Before I go on, I want to make sure that I give you a proper farewell. I don't know when Salvador could take me away."

"Is Salvador the name of the creature?"

"Yes."

"Well, then I would like to say thank you, Korin. You really made my life more enjoyable with the three visits you've given me. I suppose you visited me four times with the day I gave birth to Sean, but I didn't see you, so I wouldn't count that as a visit. You've clarified things for me in my life, and you've been a comfort to me when I was alone. Thank you for that. Thank you for your presence. Thank you for your kindness. Thank you for your time. I don't think I have ever been more grateful to a single person like I am to you, and we've only met each other three times. Perhaps it is because you already know so much about me as a fan of my work, but, even without that, I think you truly are a kind person. You've guided me through life with your words, and you were always more interested in me as a person than as an actress. You saw me for who I am, and you showed your love for God to me. Thank you."

"My goodness. I was going to thank you first, but I guess this way works better, too. I still think I could have done more for—"

"Enough, Korin. You have done more than enough for me. You didn't have to, but you visited me twice after our first encounter, and that's more than I could want from you. You did wonderful things for me with our conversations. Thank you."

"Well, now I feel a bit pressured to say something intelligent or amazing, too. I was going to say that I hope you enjoy your life with God forever and even more so when your time comes. Wait, that sounds cruel of me to talk about your death. I'm sorry. I don't know what I was thinking. More importantly, I feel sad at the thought of leaving you, but I'm beyond glad to have met you. I tell myself that I'll see you in heaven, so I shouldn't be too depressed to say farewell, but I get attached to people more easily than other people seem to. I look forward to the time when we'll be able to see each other in heaven with God and Jesus."

"I understand. Thank you, Korin," she says with a peaceful smile. "Now, what do you think of my descriptions on the paper?"

He looks down at the paper in the light, but suddenly he cannot see the words. He asks the woman if there is a power outage, but he looks up to see Earth in front him. It continues to sink, already about seven eighths into the unknown liquid.

Korin puts the paper in his pocket. He stares at the world. He is tired. He is hurting, and he finds no solace. Salvador speaks, but Korin does not listen. His heart and mind are not set, and he feels lost. He walks across the large tortoise shell towards the darkness, unafraid of liquid Time. Salvador tries to move his fins to block Korin's path, but they are pitifully short. Nothing stops Korin as he steps off.

Cornerstone

It's not fair to love people who commit suicide. I see others seeking pleasures of the world but abandoning those in need of love. I may rejoice to do God's work in loving others, but my heart cries out in pain and anger against the people of this world. Meanwhile, those in pain kill themselves. It's life. I just thought there would be more.

Good to you who know about God and realize the difficulty of loving others. Even the devil knows. Now will you do anything about it? Will you play Creator?

"You are my first best friend, Korin. Thank you for standing up for me," said a friend who was once bullied.

"Korin, you didn't know? She died two years ago. I thought you knew, but thank you, Korin, for the stories you shared about her and for listening to me. It means so much that you still care about her even though you haven't seen her for four years. No one else has mentioned her since her funeral," a female elementary classmate had said.

"We've had our disagreements in the past, and although you left me for being a jerk to everyone, you did return. No one around here can talk like you and I did about life. They are all so preoccupied on fleeting things while you and I accompany each other. Thank you," said Korin's best friend.

"Thank you for loving my daughter, for teaching her. She

desperately wanted to leave until you came along and changed everything. Now she begs me to go early to meet you and calls you her Wall-E," said Esum's mother.

"Thank you, Wall-E. You are my best friend," said Esum.

Multitudes of voices thank Korin as he sinks deeper in liquid Time.

"Stop. Please stop saying that I helped all of you. There are too many of you I want to help," Korin croaks as he sinks into the perpetual abyss.

"They can't hear you. These are your past memories," says Salvador, swimming besides Korin.

"Stop. I have regretted helping these people. I could have done more to help them."

"They thanked you."

"They didn't know that I could have done more. I didn't know that I could've done more, and sometimes I hate myself for helping them in the first place. If I had left them alone, I wouldn't have to constantly cower in anger at myself for failing to do more to help them."

"But you still helped them. You cannot do everything for them, Korin. You're asking for the impossible. Not even I can do that, to look into the future and prevent their problems; that's why I'm here to offer you a chance to stop anyone from ever going through that pain again."

"I'm scared," Korin whispers.

He cringes, casting out from the depths of his soul an uncontrolled, cacophonic echo of incredibly cold, candid cries from his inner core. They course throughout his conscious concentration and constitute to his anxious consternation. There is a respectful silence before Salvador cautiously speaks.

"You may not want to hear me speak, but remember to put aside that which prohibits your growth."

"How can I push you aside?" Korin croaks.

"I have friends. They entrusted in me their memories, sufferings, and lives up until they perished, but they will die forever if I give up. What makes you think I'll let you stop me?

"Korin, kill your fear. Get up. When my kind fears something, it is because they see the whole picture and are afraid of how to achieve their goal. Their fear blinds them from seeing the details that create a goal. Take step by step, detail by detail, to achieve a goal. Can you create a picture without details? Can you create anything if you allow fear to keep you from starting? If failure happens, bounce back up.

"Then you have the other case, when my kind focuses only on the intricate details, failing to see how they correlate to form bigger concepts. Can you see a picture if you are focused on one dot among an ocean of limitless dots on the canvas?"

Korin opens his eyes towards the dark figure of Salvador, whose eyes are closed so as not to blind Korin. Korin is not wet, yet he sinks as one does in water.

"Korin, you must see the whole picture. I am killing your people to save my kind. The details are the survivals of you and one other person. Choose quickly. Kill your anxiety and accept your conditions. I will not stop. My kind will create a foundation and reach farther to create our legacy. Your people had their time, and it is about to end."

Salvador waited patiently, but time is fading, so Salvador speaks, "Your people do not realize this, but each of you creates your own sense of loneliness, refusing to appreciate what you have in want of something you do not achieve, and then what? If you do achieve your goals, you all feel lonely again. You all repeat the cycle and keep going for something else until dead."

"Is the woman I talked to different?"

"Yes. I learned about her when I saw the horrors of World War II. There are some exceptions, people who are kind, including you and the woman, but I cannot save them all. Besides, she has already passed in your world, and I cannot bring her back to life. She had a purpose to help people, just like you and I do. She still hurt, however, from loneliness, but her happiness was just a feeling to her alone. Inside, her soul was ultimately joyful to serve God in the purpose that He had given her, and I believe it continues to rejoice in heaven. She was not always happy, but that did not matter because of her inner joy to serve God. Such people like her have rewards awaiting them in heaven."

"How do you face your loneliness, Salvador, as the last of your kind?"

"I am not alone," Salvador says with a tinge of anger.

"Why did you let me time travel one more time?"

"I am against revisiting the past through time travel, so I prevented you from time traveling while you were on my shell in the Time Realm. Then, God commanded me to allow you one more opportunity to time travel, so I let you go once more."

The darkness is disrupted by a blood yellow explosion from their left under the body of liquid Time. Suddenly, Korin feels a force kick his back towards Salvador's shell. Korin hits the creature's back, urging it to take him away from the explosion, but it stays, illuminated in light. Korin's mouth drops open as he looks at its enormous dark brown shell, bigger than a sperm whale. Salvador swims around Korin and covers him with its flippers as a bombardment of forces pound upon his shell. After several minutes, there is silence in a yellow red surrounding. Korin frees himself from the flippers, marveling from a distance at a burning extraterrestrial body in liquid Time. He assumes it is Kra and remembers Earth. He looks back and sees it sinking.

Everything vanishes in pitch blackness.

Salvador whispers in pain, "We have reached the deeper parts of the Time Realm where we can spend a lifetime and still return to the shallower parts as if no time at all had passed. I will need to recover here. The more we travel through time by sinking in liquid Time, the more vivid the past becomes. Earlier you heard your memories, but here you will invisibly revisit the *past* with an incapability of affecting it."

They stop sinking as the entire region becomes Korin's bright, childhood living room. He cannot tell that he is still in the dark Time Realm apart from the strange sensation of floating above the smooth, wooden floor. An infant Korin laughs and plays with his parents and sister. None of them notice a small portion of Salvador's gigantic shell floating through the room while the rest of it is hidden outside the room.

"It has been prophesied," Salvador says to the older Korin, "that a boy will visit the Time Realm and teach my kind a lesson. My kind referred to him as 'the Observer' or 'Observer,' for he would be an alien observing our creation. You are Observer."

Before Observer, or the older Korin, responds, they sink through the wooden floor and farther away from the living room until it disappears. They float and observe as Korin's bedroom appears from his old home that he had walked to before this whole adventure started. The four-year old Korin hesitates to leave his bed at night. Observer immediately remembers his loneliness. Korin cries, unaware that Observer is crying with him.

Observer sinks to the next scene while Salvador recovers beside him. They see Korin push his mother Hanul. Observer tries to stop Korin, but his hands go through him in vain. Observer cries as he floats, helpless to help his mom from himself.

He then observes an unfamiliar scene in which Hanul comes home from the market and opens his door to find the room empty. She searches the apartment and calls him, but his phone vibrates in his room. She panics alone. She calls Wright and tells him to look for him while she helplessly waits and hyperventilates. Though Observer knows he cannot help, he tries to hug his mom. His arms go through her, and he breaks down into tears while trying to hug her again and again. His heart tugs at him as he sinks through the floor and desperately reaches for her hand, but it disappears above the wooden floor. Observer swims up, but Salvador stops him, saying that it is pointless to go back. Observer observes the dark, oppressive floor that blocks Hanul. They sink until the room disappears.

Observer floats through the past and realizes his ignorance towards his parents. He observes his first best friend, Nick Lee, as he befriends Korin in the third grade through a game of tag. He sinks to the next moment when Nick bullies a boy named Ben Kang for being overweight, but Korin stops Nick and befriends Ben. Observer sees several moments of Korin growing older and stressing over how to be friends to both of them before their sixth grade year ends, while Nick continues to be hostile to a depressed Ben. Korin avoids asking for help because the immature supervisors punished all three of them without caring for details. Korin does not tell his parents or his favorite teacher Ms. Song about Nick because he wishes that there would be a way to stop him without involving any punishment.

Observer watches Korin cry over his friends and pray that God would help them. Korin sleeps, and Observer sees Korin's dream. Korin feels a bald head and realizes that he is in someone else's body.

He sees through the person's eyes that the person is in bed in a dark room, while the blinds to a window above the bed cover all but a sliver of sunlight. Korin feels the person's urge to go outside, but it drains out of the person with a sigh. Korin looks with the person to the room's door where three adults are talking. The person seems to have no thoughts on this as if it is normal, but Korin assumes that the crying woman is a mother hugging her husband as they listen to a doctor. The person looks back to the sunlight and feels slightly better.

A powerful sense of nostalgia fills Korin as he hears the person's thoughts: "I wish I could see Korin again."

Korin realizes that he heard a girl's voice as if she had spoken, even though he only heard her thoughts. He realizes that he is in a girl's mind as she remembers him being a silly, awkward, but sweet sixth grade boy. Korin feels a tear roll down her cheek and opens his eyes.

Observer watches Korin sit up and pause in confusion. Observer sinks away as Korin's eyes widen in an epiphany. Korin prays that nothing bad happens until his drowsiness overtakes him.

The Observer floats and watches Korin sitting in Ms. Song's classroom the next day. Korin sees a girl reading at a separate table to his left. He waits at his desk during free time, wondering when the bell will ring for recess so that he can find Ben before Nick bullies him. The rest of his classmates in his table left to talk with others. He pushes the thought aside, however, saying that he is tired of worrying about them for almost four years and that they could handle a recess without him. He is more confused about the girl beside him. She looks up, repeatedly blinking and squinting her dry eyes. Korin marvels at her brown eyes and intimate smile, wondering why they seem different from those of other kids. She notices him, freaks out, and sporadically shuts her book. She gasps in sorrow and flips through the pages to find her place. She softly glares at him and says, "Stop staring at me."

Korin jumps away to the edge of his seat like a panicked monkey, so she smiles slightly. Several classmates laugh, while others chatter about rushing out to get the best basketball or meeting up at a tree to talk about Spongebob. The classmates tease Korin as he blushes and says, "It's not what you think. I was just waiting for recess to start and happened to see you, Hang."

"Lies. The least you could do is admit that you're a creep."

"What? I'm not a creep. I was just wondering why you were blinking so much."

"Oh, my eyes were dry from reading." She pauses in reflection and asks, "What do you do besides staring at me? Wait," she says with a blush, "is that my jacket? You're a complete creep."

Korin's face further reddens as he says, "No, this morning I was swinging on the monkey bars for fun when I saw that you left it after swinging. I was going to ask you if it was yours."

"See? You are a creep. How else would you know that's my jacket?" she teases as Korin hands her the black jacket. Korin defends himself in embarrassment, while other classmates laugh. She notices his nervousness and adds, "I'm just kidding. We've been classmates for years, so of course you know what my jacket looks like, and I saw you at the monkey bars."

"Does that mean you're a creep?" Korin laughs.

"What? No. I…gah, oh my gosh. You…gah whatever." she stutters with a smile. She laughs even more at Korin's confused face as his eyes debate and then decide to ask her what she said. She pauses and wonders why Korin seems more eager than usual to talk to her. "Geez," she says with an embarrassed smile. "I was trying to make you feel better because you seemed worried that I thought you were a creep. I know you're not a creep. Thanks for giving me my jacket."

Alice Joo, Hang Lai's friend, walks to them from her seat across the classroom just as Hang says her last two sentences. "What? A creep? You don't have to worry about that, Korin!" she says with a laugh as everyone looks at Korin's red face. He moves to cover his face with his arms and the table when he notices that Hang has already done so. He wonders why she would be embarrassed when Alice was putting him on the spot. "Hang, you okay?" she says, unaware that everyone is still watching, though her voice is quieter. Hang looks up at everyone, quickly covers her face, and whispers that she is fine. "What you talking about, girl? Your face is all red!" Alice says, her voice growing even louder than before.

"Alice, your voice is too loud," Korin says.

"Oh, sorry," she says, noticing that everyone is watching and feeling embarrassed.

"It's okay," Korin reassures her. "What's up?"

"Nothing, I was just bored, so I came over. Let's hang out at the blacktop, Hang."

Hang looks up, her face still red as she nods and says, "Sure."

Ms. Song asks everyone to return to their seats, with ten minutes to spare until the bell rings for recess. Alice says farewell as the rest of the class resumes their conversations. Korin looks to his teacher smile at him from behind Hang's desk. He wonders if she did that on purpose to break off the attention, and he thanks her with a smile. Then he looks away as he realizes that she was there when Hang joked that he was a creep. He quietly sits and pretends to look at some math notes that he already knew so that his face can calm down from feeling embarrassed. After a minute, he looks back at Ms. Song, who watches over the class from her desk and then returns to her papers.

Korin wonders why Hang seemed to be in pain when she looked up and asks quietly, "Hang, do you need to go to the nurse's office?" while looking at Ms. Song who seems to avoid listening though she can easily hear them.

"No, it's okay. My head just hurts sometimes." He pauses and feels helpless. "Are you okay?" He looks at her with confusion until she adds, "Your face was pretty red."

His eyes widen as he says, "No, it wasn't. Not as much as yours."

Her face immediately reddens to his surprise as she moves to cover her face at the table but comes back up with a change of mind. "I'm joking, but you—y—you really are a creep, aren't you?" she teases with a smile.

"What do you mean? I sit right next to you!" he whispers while making small, flustered, funny gesticulations towards her chair. "We're like three feet away. I would have to be super narrow-minded to not notice you."

"That's not *right* next to me," she says with a gentle laugh, "and why don't you just say a yard?"

Korin drops his head with a sigh and nods with a smile. They quietly laugh as Korin looks at her open book. "Which *Harry Potter* is that?"

"How did you know this was *Harry Potter*?" she says, eyeing him with playful suspicion.

"Well, it's bigger than the other books we read, and you closed your book, so I saw the cover, but I don't know which book it is."

"Oh, yeah, it's the fifth one. I'm still waiting for our library to have the sixth one, even though it came out some time ago. Do you read it?"

"Yeah, but I only finished the third one so far. I think I remember seeing you read the first one when we were in the same class before. You read pretty quickly! Those books are huge."

"Yeah, they take up time," she says as she pauses. Korin looks with surprise, as though her expression and tone suddenly grew wiser, knowing something he did not. "I don't know what else I would do in my free time, though."

Korin pauses and says, "What do you do in your free time, besides reading?"

She looks at him and then her table. Korin feels shivers as she seems to look through the table at a memory he cannot see unlike in his dream of her. He pauses, wondering if he said something wrong and hurt her feelings. "Wait a minute!" she says in quiet revelation. She laughs at Korin, who jumped in shock and hit his knee on the table. "Sorry I scared you," she says, still laughing, "but you're like a monkey, jumping and climbing monkey bars! Anyways, you didn't answer my question earlier. What do you do in your free time? You should answer my question before I answer yours."

"Oh, right. I think for most of my day. Sometimes I read. I like to think about God, family, what it would be like to have a wife, and life in general. Otherwise I just watch a little television or scooter in my neighborhood. I also like to play handball outside against my garage or build LEGO sets."

"What about Lun? What's it like having an older sister?"

"She's okay. She's pretty loud sometimes. I've always had an older sister, so I don't know how to explain what it's like because I don't have an experience to compare it with. You have sisters, too, right?" She gives him a funny look, so Korin pauses and looks down at the carpet floor to her confusion. He mumbles, so Hang asks him to speak a little louder. "I…saw you walking home with two girls…." Hang grins as Korin quickly adds, "My mom was driving me home, and I looked out the window like I usually do and saw you with your sisters, I think."

"Yeah, I have two younger sisters. I get what you mean about describing what it's like to have siblings. For me, it's sort of difficult. I have to be responsible, but sometimes…I wish I could help more."

Korin wonders why she often pauses and seems more mature than him, particularly when she reflects. He then asks, "So what do you do in your free time?"

"I just read and spend time with my family. Sometimes I play with Alice, but these days not as much because I'm busy sometimes or she's busy when I'm not, so I read. Reading is my life. If I run out of books, I just reread them." She stutters at Korin's puzzled expression, "W-what? Don't you reread books?"

Korin pauses, wondering if he is causing her to stutter, and he calmly asks, "Don't you just read once and move on to the next book? Rereading takes more time."

"It does…. I think it's worth it, though. I notice different things each time I reread. It helps me think about things that I might not see otherwise."

"Well, you have a life ahead of you, right? Maybe one day you can see some of those things yourself if they exist in the real world. Is there somewhere you want to go?"

"I'm not sure. I don't think I would be able to go even if I knew," she says, looking down.

"Don't think like that. You don't know that for sure," he says with his awkward gestures as she laughs.

"Do you have somewhere you want to go?"

"Oh…, uhm…." Korin blushes as he notices Hang grin, and he quickly says, "Okay, I haven't really thought about it, but I think that's because I like being where I am. I've been to Korea, and it's nice because I get to visit family there and travel around, but I like being here because I grew up here, so after visiting Korea I don't think much about going to other places. Of course, when I'm in Korea, I like being there, too, and I long to see God in heaven."

Hang nods and repeats, "You haven't thought about another place because you like where you are." Korin wonders why the way she says those words sounds completely different from how he said them as she continues, "Maybe that's true for me, too," and smiles.

Korin sighs in relief that her pensive gloom is gone and says, "How is your head?"

"It still hurts." Korin slightly frowns to her surprise. She knows that he is kind, but she did not think that he paid much attention to her, so she says, "I feel much better, though." Korin looks at her in disbelief, but she smiles and says, "Thanks." Korin involuntarily makes a noise of confusion as she laughs. "Even though you're not a creep, you notice things about me more than others do."

"Stop talking like that," he says to her alarm. "You talk as though you're alone. You're not alone. You have two sisters, your parents, the class, and I'm literally three—o-one yard away from you."

He blushes, for he began confidently and then stuttered in a comprehensible mumble when he remembered to say one yard. He worries that he was rude. Hang stares at Korin in a momentary pause for reflection and involuntarily widens her smile to a beautiful laugh, different from the previous ones. She meant her laughs before, but this one is wholehearted and fills her eyes with light and delight. Korin laughs with her.

"Thanks, Korin."

"For what? I just talked with you. Anyone can do that."

"But few do."

There is a silence between them amongst talking classmates who are unaware of them. Ms. Song is looking at papers, but Observer notices her glancing at them with a sad smile.

"Well, thanks for talking to me, too," he says, reflecting about his lonely childhood, "for the same reason."

"What were you thinking about just now?"

"Huh? Are you a psychic?" Korin says in shock. Hang laughs, and Korin continues, "I was just thinking about having to wait at my church for about an hour every Sunday for my mom and sister to stop talking. All the kids would be gone by then, so I was usually alone. Then again, God is with me, so I was never alone, but at the same time I was. It's not bad sometimes, because even at home I would just think, so it was a little better to think outside and walk around, but sometimes it's not nice.... What do you think about when you pause, like when you said that reading takes time and then looked as if you were remembering something in the past?"

"Sounds lonely," she says empathetically. "I just think about what life is like in the end. It's an interesting thing to think about. Do you think about it?"

"Yeah, but that's...well, I guess there can be different reasons for thinking about the end. Like for me..., actually I don't want to bore you with my story. It won't take too long, but I think it's long enough to bore people." She says she wants to listen, so Korin continues, "When I was four...."

Hang holds back a laugh and says, "Sorry, I didn't think you'd start that far back. Keep going, though, I want to hear."

Korin laughs in embarrassment and says, "Oh, yeah, sorry. I don't know why, but I just start there."

Hang nods in acceptance and attentively waits with a smile. Korin nods and shares his story. By the time he finishes, Ms. Song has stopped working and was listening while overseeing the classroom.

"Wow, that's quite a story," Hang says. I didn't know you thought so much." Korin blushes, for this is the first time someone appreciated his story. "Well, I'm glad you're alive." Korin observes her reflect as she says, "Thanks for sharing. I never would have learned from you if you hadn't shared. It's good to be alive."

"How about you? What's your story?"

She pauses, her eyes debating with herself, and she shakes her head with a soft reply, "I don't think you would be interested. My life is pretty boring. You don't have to worry about it."

Korin pauses, wondering if she looks a little skinnier than he remembered, but he decides not to mention it. "What are you going to do on the blacktop with Alice?"

"I don't know. She'll probably talk about a bunch of stuff, and I'll talk with her. She's energetic sometimes, but she's a nice friend."

Korin nods and wonders what he will do during recess. He usually checked on Ben to make sure he and Nick were not fighting, but lately nothing happened. Ben would be fine playing handball with other kids who didn't care who they played with, and Nick would probably be busy playing tetherball. He decides to have fun and asks Hang if they can play tag with Alice and some other classmates. She agrees and asks him what he wants to become. Hang is surprised that he does not want to be a director, playwright, or actor like he was for the school play. He says he wants to write novels even though he does not like his writings or know what to write about so far.

"Maybe you can write about your memories with family and friends."

"Can I write about you as a friend?" She blushes and consents, so he says, "Okay! Don't expect it anytime soon, though. It'll probably be years from now. I'm still not sure what memories I would write about."

Hang pauses, her smile fading. "I don't know if I'll be able to read it if it'll take years." She looks up at Korin's worried countenance and wonders why he somehow seems to know about her sickness, but she quickly says, "It's okay, though. Take your time. Your writing might be better when you take your time," she says with a reassuring smile. "I'm sure you'll figure something out. You did well with the play."

"I'll make sure to finish it if I can. As for the play, Ms. Song and our classmates helped me, and it was just a seven-minute skit."

"I still think it was impressive. You did most of the work behind the scenes. You're a good leader, though I'm sure there are some things you can improve on. We're young, though, so we all have something to learn. That's youth, I guess."

"You suddenly sound old."

Hang blushes and gestures, "No, I do not." They laugh, and she asks, "What do you think youth is?"

"I think it's making the most of each opportunity for God's glory, not giving up on an opportunity even if you think you don't have much time left in life, because you never know how much time you'll really have until it's gone." Hang pensively nods but blushes as Korin grins and opens his mouth to say old again, but he stops and laughs with her instead.

The bell rings, and they go outside and play tag for twenty minutes. Korin runs and notices that Hang is slower than usual, but he makes sure not to let her tag her anyways. It would be too obvious that he let her tag him if he got tagged.

Korin decides that he had a bad, meaningless dream last night and imagined that the girl in his dream was Hang. Observer sinks to the next day. Korin enters the classroom and greets Ms. Song. His smile disappears as he shivers. Hang's seat is empty.

Observer floats as Korin runs to Alice at the end of the school year and asks where Hang is.

"Hang is homeschooled."

Observer sinks and sees a tenth grade Korin remember Hang and ask Alice about her. Alice pauses and says with sorrow, "You didn't know? She died three years ago, Korin."

The bell rings. Chemistry class begins. Forgotten feelings of helplessness flood in as he recalls his dream and holds in his tears in the middle of the classroom, clenching his fists and momentarily bending his head towards his notebook. Korin holds back tears as he had often practiced in Drama classes, but he hates that he does so.

Observer, however, cries.

Observer sees himself from a few months ago. Korin walks twelve miles in semi-formal apparel because formal apparel in the morning heat is unnecessary pain. He ponders about Hang and life and death. He wanted to visit her grave last year when he heard that she had passed, but he had no way of going without explaining the whole situation to his parents, which he preferred to keep to himself as a private matter. His junior year, he realized that he could start walking before dawn to her grave and return home before his parents get worried early in the afternoon, so he walks. After nearly three hours, he reaches the cemetery and enters an office. A woman kindly shows him a map and explains how to find a grave in spite of his sweat and confusion, and he walks alone to Hang's grave. He takes out the seventh *Harry Potter* book and mutters the resolution in case she never finished it. He looks at her picture on her plaque and marvels with sorrow, remembering her smile and features as though his memory of her was wonderfully corrected and reminded to think, "Yes, how could I forget? Of course she looks like that. She's beautiful." Korin pauses and silently thinks, "She was beautiful." He thanks her for encouraging him to read and write as a friend. He apologizes that he did not talk to her more while he still could. He does not cry, but he walks six miles back towards home before his legs give out. He calls his mom and asks her to pick him up, saying that he was at a service. At home, he takes a long bath.

"Salvador, it's strange, that I distract myself with useless things and pretend that they're important, only to forget what's really important, like what I learned that day. Death teaches me to accept my eventual death and enjoy life in God with and for others while I still can, just as Hang enjoyed books and being with her family."

Salvador does not reply as Observer sinks and sees Nick and Ben as they grow and continue to live life. They eventually reconciled after several complications, while Nick and Ben both thanked Korin for being their true friend.

By this time, Observer has seen many joys and sorrows of his past, including ones involving Sophia, Marsha, and his home church, but he turns to Salvador and says, "I know you're recovering and that we're deep in the Time Realm where we can experience the past, but why am I seeing this? I feel like there's another reason why we're here when there's so much going on above us."

Salvador nods and answers, "Each pain is distinct, so I will never fully understand your pain or you mine. Still, you said that you understood what I meant when I said that I would think about memories for two hours. We are here because I wanted to see if you really understood what it is like to dwell in memories both painful and joyful in spite of the business above us. I am not disappointed, but I agree that we should return soon to the shallower parts of this realm. It is vain to stay here and dwell in nostalgia for the past, because our nostalgia is a mere yearning that cannot be fully satisfied here. Nostalgia can only be satisfied at our true home with Christ in heaven. We can't do anything to change the past or know what could have happened because we are not God, but we can do something about the future. You can, for example, do what you want to do: apologize to and hug your parents while you still can. You can visit Sophia like you promised. You can go to Hang's younger sister and learn more about what happened while getting more closure for both of you. Although you cannot know what would have happened if Hang read a book you wrote about your loved ones including her, you can finish that book and give it to those people you wrote it for. The other reason why we are here is that, once I realized something about you and myself, I realized that there is one more thing you must remember, but we must go deeper. We have just arrived to this place. After this, we will go."

Observer says that he cannot do the things Salvador said because he can only choose one person to live with him, but before he finishes, Observer's blood chills in loneliness.

"Chase me."

Korin is confused by the sudden request from a little girl he had never met, but she asks him to chase her again. He looks into her hopeful eyes, puts away his confusion, and consents. She beams with infectious, radiant joy and jogs away with her short legs. He walks quickly with long legs. She turns around, worried that she is alone, so he smiles to comfort her. Her eyes reflect his smile as she screams a gorgeous river of sound, a laughter only God could create.

After a few seconds, she sits on a chair, sets up another beside her, and gently pats on it for him to sit. She cowers with hesitation, fearing that the motion disrespects an older person, but she grins when Korin sits. She explains that she had wanted to meet him before but was afraid that he would not have time for her because he was often surrounded by other kids who wanted to play with him, but this time he was alone, so she took the chance and became friends with him. Korin listens to her panting and talking while she twiddles her fingers in nervous excitement, but he lets out a thunderous laughter when she says they are friends. She jumps, startled, and laughs, too. She asks if they are friends, so Korin assures her that they are. She grins and says that he is her best friend. They talk until her mother arrives and smiles to see them laughing together.

Observer sinks. He did not expect to smile. Salvador observes Observer and asks him why he is smiling.

"You asked me why I would want to die for this world that hurt me. When I experienced that loneliness again as a child, I remembered that it's not fair. It's grace. I deserve to die, but by the grace of God through Christ redeeming me, I live. He gave me greater grace in saving me so that I can overflow with grace and forgive others. That's why I would die to save this world. I can't forget what those kids said to me unless I have brain damage. Of course I will remember, but I remind myself that I forgave them, pray that God would save them, and leave my anger to God whose justice is greater than mine and may even save them.

"As for my mother, I have to remember that I cannot know what could have happened if I was a better son, but I can do something now about the future. I just wish I learned this before you came, because now it seems I really can't do anything but pray. Then again, that's more than enough. Eventually we'll both be dead, and I can rejoice in God with her forever.

"As for Hang, I still don't know the reason why she died. I know she died of cancer and that death in this fallen world is part of Man's punishment, but I can't make sense of why I had that dream of her before she died. Perhaps there isn't a reason, but I realized that there is a purpose to this pain, that there is hope that God works this and all difficulties for good. I miss Hang. Because of her, I learned to enjoy life by making the most of my life living with and for others while I can. Plus, she helped me see the joy of rereading a book.

"Lastly, I learned from Esum that I must embrace my weakness. I haven't been able to let go of her and my feelings for her were my idols. I realized that, as a kid, I don't know anything about working at a job, saving enough money to raise a family, and putting God first. I thought I put God first because I knew the verse, but now I realize that seeking God first goes hand in hand with enjoying the world for what it is in its right place, far below God. I depended on myself for so long, so God allowed me to have a broken heart so that I could realize my idolatry and learn to depend on God. It's in my weakness that I realized how vast, personal, and powerful God's grace is.

"As for the many dreams I had of people dying like the pastor's cousin and a girl who seems to have been kidnapped for sex trafficking, I've tried so hard to keep track of each vision and derive meaning from them because I was worried that I might let someone else die like Hang. I realize now, however, that some dreams might just be pointless. If they mean something, I'm sure God will make it clear to me.

"The only thing that makes all of this pointless is that the world as I know it will be gone."

"I understand." Salvador pauses. "What's on your mind? Have you counted the cost of discipleship? The Gospel of Luke says, 'If anyone comes to me and does not hate his own father and mother and wife and children and brothers and sisters, yes, and even his own life, he cannot be my disciple.'"

Observer reflects as a scene forms. He tears up as his father cares for an infant Korin.

"Father...my earthly daddy. I hurt you. I apologize for not loving you well. When I became obsessed about Esum, I grew irritable and frustrated that I could not have my own way. You were closest to me, so you suffered the most because of that. In my anger I grew cold and detached, but I never realized how much I hurt you. That's why you became cold and detached, too. Lun wasn't much help either, but on my part I failed to love you, especially after we moved from my childhood home. I hated moving and blamed you. Then I lost Esum and hated life itself. I'm sorry I hurt you.

"I remember your love for me, how you danced with me when I was little, tickled me, smothered me with kisses, let me slide off a makeshift cardboard slide on your stomach when we couldn't afford a slide, bought me toys and games and movies, and let my head bounce off of your stomach. I know you didn't mean it when you told me to leave, but I cried as I packed up my emergency equipment and left. I realized that I loved you still because it hurt that you told me to leave, even through the phone. I realized that, while I'm still a kid in high school, I'll need your help. If I marry, then I will hold fast to my wife and leave you, but I will still keep in contact every now and then because I love you. When you and mommy are too weak to care for yourselves, I will care for you two. I just wish I could see you one more time, to apologize and thank you before it all ends. I love you."

Hanul appears and laughs with Wright and Korin. "Mother, you worry too much, but I love you. I don't think there's much left to say. I've already made my love for you clear."

Lun appears and plays with Korin. "Lun, I'm glad to have you by my side. Of course, there were times when you made life difficult for me, and I hurt you, too, but that's because we sinners grew up together. I'm sorry for the times I hurt you. Despite our conflicts, I was comforted to know that I have a sibling. We act silly with each other and make stupid sounds for fun at home. We get in each other's faces until we get annoyed with each other, but that's all part of our relationship. We've helped each other with opportunities, and I'm grateful that God used you to bring us to our home church. If you didn't exist, I would have been lonelier than I already was in many ways. We learned about our home church because your friend invited us, so I literally would not be where I am today without you. I thank God for you and our parents. I love you, dear sister."

Salvador nods as they sink away from the scene.

"If the world ends, I won't get to marry a beautiful, godly woman. Ever since I was four I've wanted a wife, which back then was someone I can love and be loved by. Now I wish I could date, court, engage, marry, and love her for who she is, just as I see the lovers do in the Song of Solomon. I'm sure we would fight because we're sinners, but I would want to fight fair. I want to love her as Christ loved the church, which would be very difficult.

"If I was in front of my future wife, I want to tell her this: I want to provide for you, protect you, and build you up as nobody else can because only I will enjoy the privilege of knowing you better than anyone does besides you and God. I want to give all of myself to you, and that means you'll be the person who can and probably will hurt me the most because I care about what you say. Still, I want to know you and be known by you. I love you more today than yesterday, because there is always more to learn about you. In other words, there is always more to love about you. From the moment I start dating you, I will never be alone with another woman besides my blood-related family members in any circumstance. Over the years, I will have known your godly character from many dates and times spent with you, so I will trust that you will never place yourself in a situation alone with a man in which Satan can tempt you. I hope to continue to date you even in marriage. Thank you for encouraging and helping me, for being a lovely stay-at-home mom who nurtures our children because I remember how much of a blessing it was to have my mom at home to care for me. Love is not just a feeling; it's a commitment, so I want to worship God and grow old with you. I want to be with and for you for better and for worse and till death do us part. Then I want to reunite with you and all our loved ones in eternity and worship God in the fullness of his glory and grace in heaven. I want to look with gentleness, passion, and compassion into your beautiful eyes and remind you often through my words and actions of serving you that I love you.

"Future children, I wish I could teach you the gospel as your father and help your mother nurture you. Of course, there would be sleepless nights and many diapers as I care for your tiny, breathing bodies, but just as my parents have done that for me, I wish I could do that for you. I wanted to read you the *Narnia* series as you fell asleep, laugh at *Calvin and Hobbes* with you, and lead family devotions in the Word of God. No doubt you will be brats sometimes because children tend to be needy and helpless at first though they think they know better, but I long to tickle and bear hug and smother you with kisses before you grow too old. I wanted to see you mature into children who glorify God for who He is in the Bible. I wanted to marvel at how you looked like me and my wife, and perhaps even like our parents or grandparents. I wanted to be at your weddings and then see your children and maybe even their children if I live long enough. In the end, I wanted to see you at my deathbed and know that you would honor me with sorrowful yet joyful remembrance at my funeral. Perhaps you could even imitate my loud laugh for the people there."

Observer sees people in various scenes as they sink further.

"My brothers and sisters are those who come to Christ, hear His Word, and obey it with joy. My church teacher, John, is the brother in Christ who helped me the most throughout the years, teaching, correcting, and rebuking me in love so that I can mature more. He taught me more about the Bible than anybody else so far because he knows and cares for me. He also has faith that God will use me to do great things, which is a great encouragement. I wish I could thank him for all the sacrifices he made to show his brotherly love for me. I want to be with my brothers in Christ who have been with me through struggles, particularly Nick who has been through suicidal thoughts like I have, endured hardships and learned steadfastness in the Lord, laughed at *Calvin and Hobbes*, and prayed with me throughout the years, regardless of the physical distance between us during the more recent years of our relationship now that he is in Korea and I am in America. Our bond over the years shows me how faithful God is in keeping us alive and running after God despite the sufferings we faced apart from each other. I also want to be with the brothers from my church, to be silly with them and serious in joy at appropriate times. I wanted to get to know them more as we help our church family together.

"I also wish to grow with the sisters in Christ, particularly Mary and Martha, two godly twins. They are young, so I wouldn't call them women yet, but in terms of spiritual maturity, they are women of the triune God. When I see them, I see godly submission in being joyful hearers and obedient doers of God's Word. I see commitment in growing with others in our imperfect church. I see wisdom in knowing how to freely say no to people who may be legalistic by forcing them to do what they do not see themselves doing in God. I see godly suffering in enduring and turning to Christ in outstanding ways. They make mistakes, as I certainly do, but that means that we're human! Thankfully, God's grace abounds for us so that we may continue to grow in Christ together as we have been doing. I just wish that I could spend more time with my brothers and sisters in this life.

"As for my own life, to live is Christ; to die is gain. I wouldn't be alive if God was not real because He created me and then saved me by answering my prayer that night when I was four. God gave me all that I have and promises to reward me for my sacrifices, so in a sense I never made a sacrifice. I would rather be at home with Christ than here, but while I am here, I would want to love people here.

"Altogether, I have counted the cost. I love each of them very much, but, as a Christian, I know that I might lose all of them, just as Job lost so many loved ones and possessions. As unimaginably difficult it would be to lose all of the above, I will only follow Christ. As Job said, "I know that you can do all things, and that no purpose of yours can be thwarted." If God lets me lose everything, I will trust that the best way to gain Christ for my good is to let me lose everyone I love because God is sovereign and promises to bring to completion the good work He began in me. I doubt that I will lose everyone, but if I do, I have already counted the cost, so I will not be surprised. Of course..., I will ache and grieve in that case. Nonetheless, God in His providence works everything together for my good. He knows my pain; He cares; He's here with and for me always. During and after all the grieving, I will still worship God with joy in my salvation and the Holy Spirit with Job as an example.

"Now that you're going to kill everyone..., we'll find out if I hold true, but I know I will. I have counted the cost and follow Christ. To live is Christ; to die is gain."

Salvador pauses before he says, "Korin Hugo. Observer. Junior in high school. To think that one so young would teach me at my old age. Thank you. Now, out of courtesy, I would like to share my story."

Observer feels the shell shaking less than before. Salvador grabs him with its mouth and slowly swims up. As they swim, however, the whole region takes on a scene of immense proportions as countless other turtle-like Krans the size of sperm whales fill a desert. Some are beside machines three stories tall and wide, but those Krans vanish in the blink of an eye. Others panic as they try to destroy the machines, but they begin to fade away. Within seconds, there is no life. Suddenly, everyone returns, and this time a machine is destroyed, but still some Krans vanish and others begin to fade away.

"This is the Time War. The machines assist Krans in traveling to the past. It was originally supposed to transport people to the Time Realm where they can dwell in their memories in no time at all, but some Krans learned to manipulate time for themselves. They duplicated thousands of machines before they ended up killing each other in greed. We saw those machines explode throughout Kra due to the heat of its dying star, S'haon."

They ascend as the scene is replaced by a Kran half the size of most Krans, a couple of Krans who seem to be parents, and an elderly Kran who are behind a thick glass-like wall. They mourn as they observe other Krans carrying a coffin the size of a fully grown Kran into a different kind of machine. Observer's eyes widen when a breath of fire roars out of the machine, for he realizes that, though he cannot impact the past, he can feel the heat of the flames from behind the wall. The Krans place the coffin on an automatic platform that slowly moves the coffin into the flames before the machine's doors close.

"I am the young Kran, Observer. When I saw my grandmother cremated, I regretted all my failures in loving her. Her ashes were later placed in a beautiful jar. I wanted to go back in time and love her the way she always loved me, so for years I studied and helped form the first team of Krans to study time in order to create the Time Realm and the Time Machine. As I grew older, however, I studied ancient manuscripts, befriended Krans, married a beautiful Krana, and had two children with her. I learned to rejoice in the present, remember the past, and plan for the future.

"I realized the necessity of time and that I was chasing after wind in trying to control it. There is no way I can control time; the ashes of my grandmother prove that. By the time I realized this, my team had discovered time travel. Immediately I saw their greed and realized that time travel is a manipulation of time to play God. Just as Man hijacked God's gifts of craftsmanship and more to build the Tower of Babel, Krans hijacked God's gift of time to build the Time Realm. Rather than enjoying those gifts and glorifying God through them, they used them against God. As a result, God scattered my team and gave them multiple languages, but their evil schemes eventually lead to the war."

The scene is replaced with a young Salvador crying out in horror as he reaches out to his parents, wife, and children one last time before they fade away. The scene disappears below them as they ascend. Yellow and orange light fills the region, temporarily blinding Korin. He squints and sees Kra burning.

They ascend further until they reach the surface. Salvador opens his eyes, but they are not shining. Korin looks up at the creature's wrinkled face for the first time. He is crying.

"When I'm gone, you'll lose your power to time travel. I'll send you back to your time period and—"

"Gone?"

"—you won't remember anything from before you first time traveled. I haven't done this before, so I might not send you at the exact time that you slept on the bench at the park, but—"

"Why do you have to do that to kill my people?"

"—I should be able to send you close enough to the time you slept on the bench at your childhood park. There might be some complications for you, and I apologize beforehand in case I accidentally cause you any pain."

"Are you erasing my memories, too?"

"Yes, but only the parts of your time travels. It is time that you return to your world."

"What are you trying to do?"

"Korin, I have hope in God's choice, that He will use you to save many lives. Your impact may be just a drop, but it will be potent in the ocean of Time. Never forget your passion. Your emotional nature is your most beautiful characteristic, but it is also very dangerous if it takes over your heart. Remember that God provides His shoulder to you when you are in need if you obey Him. Remember—"

"You're not going to save your kind?"

Salvador pauses. It says, "My kind is already in the afterlife. I am being selfish in trying to relive their lives for them. They are gone."

"What's going to happen to you?"

"Remember that God knows your heart and your struggles, but

He has already overcome the world for you in Christ Jesus. Celebrate that in your soul, and know that your purpose is not vain."

"Answer me, Salvador!"

"I am the last of my kind. Do you think it is fitting that God created life with Adam, and now my world will end with me? God first created Man, and at the end, the male was the last one to die."

"No, take over my mind, Salvador. Live."

"I have not given up, Korin. I still love the Lord, and that is why I choose to die. I accept that my time has come. What we just saw was my dying planet. I suspect the technologies have melted and exploded throughout my planet due to the proximity of our star. Soon enough, I will be gone. Your time is yet to come, so I entrust my faith unto you, to save your world as I have tried to for mine. As for me, Time is running out. Today is the day to decide all days."

Korin looks at Earth, nearly submerged in liquid Time.

"How will I remember you, Salvador, if you take away my memories?"

"You won't remember me, and it is better that way. If you awake convinced of having memories of a giant tortoise with glowing eyes, people will disregard you with a disorder."

"I'd rather be ignored in their eyes than a fool who forgets you."

"I know. Nonetheless, it is better that you avoid time travel, for it is what brought about ruin in my world. I will do what I can to eradicate time travel with my death so that your people do not make the same mistakes my kind did. Even if I warn your people, I know they will fail, so this is the end of time travel and of me. I now see why God allowed for dreams but made time travel humanly impossible. I have played God for too long, and I have failed. The best that I can do is to send you back to a time before all this happened and erase your memories."

"This feels so wrong, though. I won't just let you die."

"Yet you must. That is why you were chosen. You are the Observer, and you have been faithful. No reasoning of our kind can save lives, but God will save us. I am no God, and I must kill time travel before anyone else tries to play God as I have so foolishly done so."

"What brought you to change your mind?"

"Your question of my loneliness struck me as true," he says. "Korin, I will be alone even if I put memories of my kind in the brains of your people. They will only be dead existences of memories trapped in human flesh, and it will be depressing to see such pure memories distorted by my selfish desires. They will only wander like lost souls waiting to be freed. I have no right to do that, yet I hoped that I could save them, reluctant to accept that they are in the afterlife. You reminded me of truth. Thank you, Korin." Salvador floats towards Earth. His body is almost as big as Earth, but Earth's representation in the Time Realm is smaller than the actual Earth, for Korin is almost as big as Asia. "Korin, we are in a dimension that defies your logic. That is why Earth is small, for you are in the domain of a Creator. Although my kind created the Time Realm, God is much bigger than you and I even in this dimension, and His logic is beyond our mental capacities. How much bigger God is if He were to show Himself in this Realm, and even more so when we are in our own worlds," he marvels. Salvador releases Korin from his mouth and swims under Earth. Korin sees cracks on his shell from the explosion. Salvador strains to lift Earth out of Time. Korin cannot swim, so he sinks and observes Salvador's eyes. The yellow red light from Salvador's burning planet provides enough light so that he does not need to shine light upon the world. His eyes hold the same look the woman had when she was writing words to describe Korin, but his held pain as he carried the weight of the world's sins on his back. His eyes burn with determination as Earth slowly floats to the surface. Korin realizes he can still breathe in this substance. He easily swims up without drowning, and together they push Earth up.

Korin and Salvador watch Earth fly away from liquid Time. Salvador's mouth forms a peculiar smile, as though he had not done so for centuries.

"Satan made me a deal, Korin. He said he would give me the chance to save my kind if I killed your people, and I agreed. He brought Earth closer to liquid Time so that your world would sink into liquid Time. With your world so close to me in the Time Realm, I would easily transfer all the memories, but I changed my mind. Now your world is back where it belongs. In time, it, too, will naturally submerge in liquid Time, like all planets do before they explode into oblivion in the Time Realm."

Liquid Time darkens with red. Salvador grabs Korin in his mouth and throws him up. Korin feels a soft barrier as he passes it. He is facing Salvador, who keeps smiling as an explosion consumes him. The force of the explosion is contained in the barrier as Korin yells, but he closes his mouth for air. He cannot breathe in the water as he floats up. Then, there is darkness below, as though nothing had been there a moment ago.

Korin gasps for air as he floats up in the middle of an ocean. He looks up at the bright sky riddled with serene clouds, but he cannot remember why he is there. He naturally floats on his back and looks around. He is alone.

Korin remembers a woman, but he cannot recall her name. *Sean. Was that her name? No, that's not it. Am I dreaming?*

Korin awakens on the street on his way to his apartment from the crafts service while holding an object. He cannot understand why, but he thinks he experienced something he cannot recall. Korin drops to the floor, screaming with aching legs as sudden thoughts rush through his mind. He cannot consciously grasp his memories, but the sensations they arouse pierce his soul. He throws up. His body runs with immense fervor down the street in desperation to get somewhere. He has a destination in mind, but he does not know where he is going. Overwhelming concern shrouds his mind until he drops. Drivers look at him and then move on. They had watched walkers before and forgotten them. Pedestrians, queer aliens apart from society.

Each second uncontrollably hurts him as rivers stream from his eyes. His heart feels submerged in a sea within his chest. Despite the tears, he sees visions of a woman, a baby, a burning sphere, and a figure with glowing eyes. He falls, unconscious. Nobody stops their cars.

A bell chimes. Black bell. White bells. Plastic stars and straws. A punctured Styrofoam cup. Red strings attached, holding these objects together. On the cup is a name, but his eyes are blurry from tears. Pangs of utter loneliness crush his cranium as he struggles to gasp for an escape. The boy cannot move, but his eyes are looking at the name. He remains on the floor.

"Make sure you quit quitting," Salvador whispered before he threw Korin up.

"Of course, Salvador."

The boy awakens and turns to the sky. He feels calm. Mechanical monsters roar past him, but he does not flinch.

The boy looks around to see if someone dropped an object, but he is the only pedestrian. He feels that a part of him is absent and lost. He finds himself walking straight ahead, but he does not know where. He carries the object with both hands. He believes he must protect it and return it to its owner. His body seems to know where to go, so he simply obeys.

He arrives at an apartment door. His hand reaches for his left pocket and retrieves a key to unlock the door. He marvels that he has a key and assumes this is his home. The boy opens the door to see familiar objects, but a woman rushes towards him. He does not who she is, but she has terrible energy. He senses blind rage with a tinge of evil, yet the boy feels compassion in her voice. He assumes that she is his mother, but he does not understand why she is angry. He vaguely remembers a collective cry of billions of souls, forming an unspeakable aura of horror, so that the person's yells are adorable in comparison.

"What is that?" his mother demands in Korean. The boy turns around and leaves while his mother screams, "Korin! What are you doing? Get back here!" The boy runs. He believes he must escape to somewhere, anywhere, and his body would take him there. *Korin*, he thinks. *Am I Korin?*

The boy stands at the street and looks to his left where he had come from. His mind starts to remember some buildings in that direction. He remembers a building and the word, "School." He remembers a hallway, but he cannot remember why it seems important, so he disregards it. He remembers an old woman he enjoyed conversing with, but he feels no need to talk to her again. He lets his body take him, the holy temple that God had intentionally and thoughtfully molded and breathed life into. He turns right.

He sees a crossroads and a button with an image of a figure

posing curiously. Mechanical monsters roar by, so the boy pushes the button and waits. After several minutes, the lights change, and he sees a white light in the shape of the posing figure, so the boy imitates the pose to show his thanks. He looks and sees the figure is replaced by red numbers counting down, so he runs across the street. The boy looks back and sees he has survived. He thanks God and continues onwards. He walks for a mile and then sees a fellow pedestrian. The pedestrian is jogging but seems tense as the distance between them decreases. The boy worries that the pedestrian is frightened, so he waves his hand to the man whose eyes light up. The man nods his head and smiles as they pass each other.

For a moment, the street is desolate; no mechanical monsters rush by or kill the peaceful atmosphere as the boy observes trees and bushes strategically placed about the dead concrete. He shivers as the winter air flies against him. He walks several miles and starts to ache in his legs, but his body continues forward.

The boy feels that he walked this path before. He recognizes something about the mechanical monsters and notices other people in them. They are eaten by these monsters, yet these pedestrians do not seem to mind. They barely look at their surroundings but look at the boy as though *he* is the peculiar anomaly. The boy waves to them, but they all look away. The boy shrugs and thinks they did not see him. One kid, however, waves back to him, and they share friendly smiles with each other, the only companions on the street who acknowledge each other's life. The boy wants to save the kid from the mechanical monster, but it rolls away. The boy marvels at its speed and wonders. The boy walks up to a mechanical monster that is waiting at the crossroads and asks if it will eat him, too. The pedestrian inside yells at him with sinister eyes, but the boy explains to the pedestrian that he understands the danger of this mechanical monster but still wants to be eaten so that he can move while his feet rest. He says he trusts the mechanical monster enough after seeing a kid who did not seem to be in danger. The spotlight changes, and the monster growls, zooming away. The boy returns to the sidewalk, but he hears a voice call to him. He turns to see a stranger who tells the boy to be careful on the street. The side of the stranger's beast is slightly open.

"May I join you in this mechanical monster? My feet hurt, and I get the impression that I have much longer to go."

"Where are you heading?"

"I don't know."

"I can't help you if you don't—"

Mechanical monsters make terrible shrieks behind them, so the stranger beckons for the boy to enter. The boy sees a handle at the side of the beast. He pulls it, enters the beast, closes its side, and greets the stranger as the beast moves forward.

"How do you not know where you are heading?"

"I do not know. I woke up on the street with this object. I do not remember much else."

"Are you homeless?"

"No. O beast, turn left at the next crossroads, please."

"What? You know where you're going?"

"I think so. This road looks familiar."

"Well, I have to go straight, so I don't think I can do that for you."

"Do you control this beast?"

"What are you talking about? This is a car, and yes, I control it."

"Outstanding. Will you please stop this...car? I can walk from here."

"Wait. I am not leaving you on the street if you're lost. I'll take you where you need to go. My lunch can wait. What's that cup for?"

"Thank you, and I don't know. I think I'm searching for its owner."

"Sophia?" he reads.

"No, I don't think it belongs to whoever Sophia is. I feel like I need to find the owner."

They talk about anything the boy remembers, and the stranger soon trusts the boy. Every word the boy says seems candid, and the boy does seem clueless. The stranger asks if the boy is hungry, and the boy nods. The stranger smiles and says he will buy him food before they move on. The boy replies his thanks. The stranger stops in front of a hamburger restaurant and asks the boy if he knows what a hamburger is. The boy politely asks if the stranger will teach him. The stranger smiles, says he will show him a hamburger, and walks away while the boy yawns.

When the stranger returns, the boy is gone. The stranger looks around for the boy but cannot find him. He growls, thinking the boy had robbed something, but his anger becomes worry as he sees that his money and possessions are as he had left him. The stranger checks the store and then rushes into his car, driving for several blocks in all four directions around the store to no avail. The stranger wonders what could have happened and feels the boy's absence. The boy reminded him of his mother. His mother was not clueless, but the boy had the same kindness she had, and somehow he felt a connection to the boy, as though something beyond his awareness had arranged for them to meet. He regrets not telling the boy his name so that at least one of them had something to remember by to meet each other again. He had been working on a book about his mother but was not certain of the title until he met the boy. The boy had disappeared, but the stranger could still sense his spirit, an elegant spirit. Sean smiles. That would be a good title for his book about his mother.

The boy awakens and looks around for the stranger and a hamburger. He feels tired, but otherwise his head is fine.

The boy stretches and feels bags on a stone bench next to a dead lamp. He observes the old park hidden in the winter night. He feels a peculiar sensation of something fading out of his mind as Salvador's final act takes hold in eradicating the prohibited power of time travel. The boy shivers and reaches into his pockets. He feels a paper, takes it out, and reads several words that seem to fit his characteristics. He cannot recognize whose handwriting is on the note or why he has it, but he puts it back in his pocket. The ocean that once troubled his burning chest evaporates into his visible sigh of relief before dissipating to nothing.

All time is restored as it was before Korin had first time traveled to Rome.

Korin reflects about *HER* and smiles at the thought of her smile, but he gets a rippling impression that a woman suggested he give *HER* a nickname. He remembers the name, "Esum," and nods in vague remembrance.

Korin realizes that his parents are likely to be searching for him. He cringes in disgust as he remembers that he pushed his mother. Korin takes his two bags and walks home to his family, willing to accept the consequences of his sins.

All the while, a wind chime craft, made of a cup attached to stars and bells, awaits its creator's arrival.

The Devil tempts the Observer, but the Observer and the Spirit trust in God the Father, Son, and Holy Spirit. The Devil fails. God prevails in victory and glory. Nonetheless, the Devil continues his threats.

EPILOGUE

Korin sees a familiar elder and sits next to her. She does not give signs of recognition, so he kindly treats her as he would treat a new acquaintance. Korin smiles as the seniors play Bingo with excitement, and the woman thanks Korin in German each time he updates her bingo board. He responds accordingly each time. She sits back and watches him focus on the board, intent on helping her play the game because she cannot see the numbers too well. She asks him if he remembers her.

Korin looks up with alarm and smiles, "Yes, you are Sophia. Do you remember me?"

"Yes, of course. I remember your face, but what was your name again?"

He tells her, and she says, "Korin. Yes, that sounds familiar. You came back."

"I'm sorry it took a year for me to come back."

"No, it's all right. I wasn't sure if you'd come back. You are young, so you should be busy instead of visiting me all the time. Danke, Korin."

They finish several games, and a worker announces that the volunteer session is over. Korin says farewell to Sophia, but she leans forward and beckons him to come closer. He leans forward on his chair, and she embraces him. She turns and kisses him on the cheek and laughs heartily. She thanks him once more in German. Korin smiles, bids Sophia farewell, and thanks her for her time. She opens her mouth to ask him to visit again, but she decides against it, afraid that the request would burden him. She doubts that she would ever see him again now that he is going off to college. She watches his back as he leaves with sorrow, but he turns around at the doorway and waves again. She smiles and waves back, but she looks down as he starts to turn. She believes it is their last time together, so she does not want to remember his back; she wants to remember his smile. In this world, they never meet again.

Korin stands shocked in his school hallway. Two years ago, he heard that Hang passed in the seventh grade, yet she seems to be laughing with girls across the hall. Korin enters his Spanish classroom and realizes that she is entering it, too. He turns to Marsha and explains his confusion, but he realizes that the girl looks a little different than Hang and is talking to juniors rather than seniors like Korin. He remembers that Hang had two younger sisters and that they were most likely in the same school district as him. Class begins, but they finish their lesson early and are allowed to socialize for some minutes before the next class.

Korin talks to Marsha, who asks him several questions about how he is doing. He left to Korea with his family for two weeks when they got a phone call that Kyeo, Hanul's mother, was found unconscious in the bathroom. They took the second earliest flight to Korea, but upon arrival, they learned that she died around the time that they boarded their flight. Even if they had taken the earliest flight, she would have officially died by the time they arrived at the Korean airport. Up until then, a machine merely kept her heart beating. Korin spent time with extended family, happily reunited with Nick, and enjoyed a conversation with a childhood friend. He mourned for his grandmother and dreamt that she was alive, that she would bring more food to him as she used to even when she had fed him the hour before. Now he has two weeks of schoolwork to catch up on for four Advanced Placement classes, one regular Physics class, and two extracurricular classes. Nonetheless, he is focused on the girl who looks like Hang. He asks Marsha if they can catch up later. She nods, and he goes.

"Did you have an older sister named...Hang?"

Beatrice looks away, her eyes slightly saddened as she quietly says yes. Korin learns that she had thought about talking to him but decided that she did not know him too well, so she stayed away when he did not talk to her, either. Beatrice looks up. To her surprise, Korin smiles widely at her in revelation of who she is. They occasionally talk during free times in class and at the hallway towards Spanish class for three weeks. Korin often greets her with sincere enthusiasm, which at first surprises her but encourages her to respond similarly.

Now that Korin appreciates Beatrice for who she is, he tells her about walking eighteen consecutive miles, the farthest he has walked so far.

"I never quite...knew what happened to Hang. Will you tell me?"

"Oh," she remarks. "You mean...sixth grade. Okay. One day, we were late to school. My sister and I went without Hang. She was at our house still, but then she fell down. She was rushed to the hospital. The doctors found a tumor. They tried to remove it, but then they left a tool in there. My parents were furious. A year later, she died."

"Okay, wait, that was a quick—"

"Okay, okay. She went to another hospital and stayed there for six months. At one point, the tumor was gone, but then it returned and grew worse. The doctors couldn't get rid of the brain tumor near her spinal cord in case it would paralyze her. She came back home after that. She didn't get better. There were a bunch of close calls. And then she finally died." Beatrice stares at Korin's sorrowful gaze soften in relief at her final words as he senses the end of Hang's pain. "Cancer runs in the ladies of my family. My grandmother and mother had stomach cancer. They're all fine. Only Hang.... My younger sister and I have a high chance of cancer."

"Is your sister a junior like you?"

"She's a sophomore."

"She must have struggled. How did you get through the loss?"

"I was the stupid fifth grader who thought, 'Why don't you pay attention to me?' I didn't really care about Hang until about sixth and seventh grade. Then I focused on her. We spent time together. I thought it was unreal. Do you know how that feels? It was weird. Someone you love dies, and you think the person is still alive. She wasn't. I couldn't believe it. I don't know. For some reason, I've recently felt guilty about not spending more time with her, so I feel really sad."

The bell rings.

"It has been really nice talking to you," Korin says, emphasizing each syllable in a reluctant departure. "We should talk more when we can...whenever that is."

Beatrice laughs and nods her head in agreement. Over time, Korin tells her about a book he plans on writing and asks for her permission to write about her and Hang. She smiles and consents, and he promises to give her a copy when it is finished.

Korin watches Hanul mourn for Kyeo. Kyeo was the only family member who believed that he would become a great director when he said he wanted to become one in elementary. Then he said he wanted to become a great writer, and she believed that he could do it. Now her ashes are in a colorful jar. Relatives argued over who gets her inheritance, but they discovered that she spent all her money for her loved ones while she lived, even though she did not expect to die anytime soon. She lived a full life.

Korin remembers what his grandfather, Seo, said to himself in Korean while mourning: "I don't know what to do for the ceremony. That's terrible..., but it's a good thing—not to know." He remembers seeing Kyeo's bloated corpse from staying in a freezer. He remembers how cold her face was when he could touch it one last time. He remembers how much he did not know, while death stared him in the face. He regrets his mistakes, including how he complained instead of thanking Kyeo for giving him food nearly every hour when he refused, but Hanul tells him that he was still a kid back then.

She says in Korean, "You were unusually kind as a kid and easy to raise up, but you were and still are a kid. Don't blame yourself. You did wrong, but it's okay. She loved you and knew you didn't mean it. She knew you were still young..., but I'm an adult. I should've done better. Korin, promise me this. Promise me that you'll remember her. Is it bad of me that her face is already hard to remember?"

She cries again. Korin promises to remember and hugs Hanul.

As soon as Korin disappears outside the Time Realm, Salvador barely manages to reverse time before the explosion of Kra engulfs him. He erases Korin's memories. He rests, waiting for the end, but his eyes shine towards a source of new ripples. Three men swim towards him, and they explain all that has happened. During the Time War, Ile Uase, who was with Salvador when creating the Time Realm, time traveled to Earth and took over the minds of three people because a Kran's brain capacity is equal to that of three adults combined. In the process, however, he was greatly weakened with severe headaches and could only make it back to the Time Realm once more if he could sense where it was, which he just did when he sensed an immense change in time. After Salvador explains what happened, Ile criticizes him for breaking his moral code against time travel for a boy but refusing to do so for his planet. Salvador almost gives in but refuses, remembering his family and Korin Hugo. Ile Uase threatens to kill him with grenades.

Salvador growls at the three men and says, "Even if you could kill me physically, you can't kill me spiritually. I would help fulfill the appointed number of martyrs before the end of all worlds, but you can't kill me either way. I'm faster than you, and I can return to Kra. The only thing you can do is deceive me. Victory belongs to God." He pauses and urges Ile, "Our planet will die soon. Please, while there is still a chance for you, repent. You have heard of Jesus Christ. You know he died on the cross for all sins of those who believe in him once and for all. Repent, receive him as Savior and Lord, and believe."

Before he can continue, Ile throws grenades, but everything goes dark. Salvador vanished to Kra. Ile yells in frustration as the grenades explode near him. Meanwhile, Salvador reflects on his family and Korin, while Ile is stuck in the Time Realm until Kra explodes.

Korin observes the sea, listening to it part as the motorboat rushes onwards towards an island. He reflects upon a dream in which he and others were escaping lava by sliding down cracked stone stairs on shields. Then he sank into the ocean and saw a giant tortoise-like creature with glowing eyes. He still does not know the reason why he had the dream, just as he does not know the reason why Hang or Kyeo died, but he learned a purpose for each occurrence. He learned from Hang and Kyeo to live with and for others while he still could, and he learned that the dream was one of the many indications for showing him his calling: to become a missionary to the unreached, unengaged people groups with a team of Christian brothers and sisters. Though nobody remembers what happened when he met the woman Audrey Hepburn, her son Sean, and Salvador, this is their story that happened and never happened. History was not altered in any way. Korin went on to learn over time what he learned in the Time Realm in a better way: God's way. He wrote books dedicated to his grandparents, parents, Lun, John, Nick, Ben, Mary, Martha, Hang, Beatrice, Marsha, Lucy who he no longer idolized as his backwards muse Esum, brothers and sisters from his church, and many more, but this is not that book. Those books are special, ones that cannot be read by the unintended audience, because they only exist from the experiences they shared together. Every gathering is a chapter; every conversation an improvised script; every laughter a poem that points to a superior, perfect Book of Life in which every millisecond or word is greater than the one before forever.

ABOUT THE AUTHOR

Walter Lee lives in America. He wrote LOTA, or Love of the Ages, as a junior in high school. Years later, he expanded it into a trilogy but later condensed it into this book. He loves to read C.S. Lewis, A.W. Tozer's *Knowledge of the Holy*, Gibson's *Living Life Backwards*, Reinke's *12 Ways Your Phone is Changing You*, and more. He also enjoys the *Narnia* series and *Calvin and Hobbes*. He writes, plays instruments, does sports, meets with friends for fun, and is dedicated to his home church. One day, he hopes to be a missionary with trusted Christian friends.

In serious joy,
In mourning, and
In all circumstances,
Always REJOICE
in the Lord!

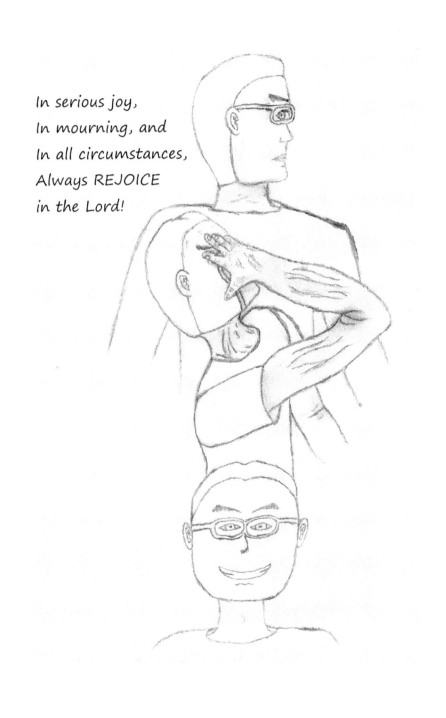

CPSIA information can be obtained
at www.ICGtesting.com
Printed in the USA
BVHW03*1044060918
526709BV00005B/18/P